SEALING DANGER
with a KISS

C.E. SAWYER

Sealing Danger with a Kiss
Copyright 2015 by C.E. Sawyer
First edition

ISBN 978-0-9861417-0-6

Publisher: Five Suns Entertainment L.L.C.

Book design by Alan Pranke

Printed in the UNITED STATES OF AMERICA

DEDICATION

To the special people in my life whose excitement, encouragement, and support helped me on through this journey. Thank you from the bottom of my heart.

CHAPTER 1

Occasionally there are nights where you go out on the town with no expectations, with no definitive plans, only the promise to yourself: I'll let the night take me. Sometimes those nights turn out to be the most memorable, the most unique, and sometimes, those nights might change your life. This happened to be one of those nights, but I didn't know it yet.

Jodi, overly confident and always on the prowl, stepped out the door at the back of the crowded bar, with me close behind, gingerly balancing both of our drinks. While tossing her flowing long blonde hair over one shoulder, Jodi surveyed the few small groups gathered by the corners of the fenced-in patio. Noticing a group of nicely dressed and professional young men, she bee lined it towards the edge of their circle. Ice and snow covered some of the cobblestone pathway, and my feet were sliding with each tentative step as I tried to follow Jodi to the corner.

Christmas lights twinkled along the thatched overhanging roof, adding shadows and light to the large patio area. They left their lights on for most of the year, even though we were well past St. Patrick's Day. Finding positives in the middle of a Midwest winter is hard, especially with extended cold periods like we have in Chicago, and nothing beats bundling up with good company, surrounded by festive lights gleaming off freshly fallen snow. However, it's hell when trying to maneuver with full drinks in your hands.

Once Jodi was satisfied that we were close enough to the guys to be noticed, but far enough away so we were not intruding, I quickly handed over her martini so I could pull my red pea coat snugly around my waist to fight off the cold. The night air was brisk, but manageable, and as all the gathered groups eagerly chatted, their breath hung in the air in tufts. Jodi dug her long fingers into her designer clutch, and pulled out a pack of filtered cigs. The pack was black and hot pink, as feminine as cigarettes could be in the dark night. The long white cigs looked delicate and dainty. I sipped my rum and diet soda as Jodi's thumb caressed the trigger of the lighter, and a few sparks fell as the flame lit up her pretty face. Taking a deep breath, she exhaled, and leaned in close to whisper.

"I'm going to see if any of these cuties will come over. I'm giving some of them a welcoming look now." She winked as I gulped my drink, trying not to roll my eyes. Jodi had the emotional maturity of a 15-year-old girl stuck in a sassy 28-year-old woman's body, which made her one of my more free-spirited friends, but also got her into trouble at times. It never ceased to amaze me that we were the same age, but we were very different. She had wild curly hair, while mine was stick-straight and almost black. People often asked if I was from Spanish descent, with my dark hair and more exotic features, while Jodi was always asked if she was Irish.

I was starting to feel the cocktails, but I still wasn't bold enough to schmooze with strangers—*very cute strangers*. As I was going in for another sip, hoping my breath didn't smell like rum in case one of the cute guys did decide to talk to us, I felt the pressure of a hand gently touching my left shoulder. I was so startled I jumped a little, and spilled my drink on the front of my coat as I turned carefully on the icy cobblestones. *Damn these spike heels.* A classically tall, dark, and handsome man was looking right at me. *Well, hello Clark Kent.* His penetrating blue eyes were sharp, but had a hint of laughter at my clumsiness. His dark features struck me even through the darkness. He was well dressed in perfectly fit dark jeans and an immaculate gray sweater, which *had to be* cashmere, and I saw the hint of his muscles beneath, all fitting together nicely on his 6'4" frame. The sweater was clinging to his bulging arms and a formidable chest. He was smiling warmly at me, while I fidgeted under his sharp gaze.

"Excuse me, could I borrow a light?" he asked, motioning to the unlit cigar he had in his other hand. Jodi had not noticed the stranger approach me, she was too busy scrolling through her phone, and making eyes at a blond Ivy League type in the middle of the group of guys.

"Um," I stammered and swallowed, trying to nonchalantly wipe the dribbles of my drink off my coat. His good looks and strong features intimidated me. My usual confidence melted away whenever I engaged with a handsome face—

and this guy was a stunner. Unfortunately, I couldn't find one single flaw in him. He looked like he could grace the cover of a Calvin Klein underwear ad.

Finding my voice, I continued, "My friend Jodi is the one with the lighter. I don't smoke, but let me grab it for you." I mustered a quick smile and turned to mouth the request to Jodi who was now talking animatedly on the phone as she inched closer to the blond Ken doll she had her eye on. She had one ear plugged with her finger to block out the noise, her nose crinkled as she struggled to get my meaning. Her eyes widened as she pointed to her lighter, and then to the guy behind me, and winked and passed me the lighter. She motioned to her phone and voiced "Russell," her flavor of last week, who from Jodi's comments I didn't think would last into next week. I nodded as she pointed towards the bar and mimed that she was going to try to move inside so she could hear better on her phone. I turned back around and passed the lighter to the dark-haired stranger.

"Thanks." He nonchalantly took a couple puffs of his cigar, and passed the lighter back. He appeared to be alone. "Where did your friend go," he asked through the noise of the crowd.

"Um, she couldn't hear her phone. She'll be back in a second." It hit me, I was alone with this man, and I was racking my brain for something else to say. He seemed to be looking at me.

Exhaling the sweet smoke from his cigar, he leaned against the fence. "I'm Will, I would love to keep you company until she gets back. My friends are inside undoubtedly doing another round of shots, which was a good time for me to take a quick break." He grinned, and I noticed the faint lines around the corner of his mouth. *Oh shoot, I think I'm staring at his mouth.* I looked down at the ground quickly in hopes he didn't notice my fixation with his perfectly curved plump lips. He nodded to his cigar, "A friend got engaged, so we're having a bit of a celebration for him tonight, thus the cigar." I liked the richness of his deep voice, and the way he drew out his words was like a long sip from a glass of vintage wine. This man reeked of class, mixed with his polo-player good looks and brains. Where was his girlfriend? How do some girls get so lucky?

"Thanks for the lighter." He was looking right into my eyes as he handed it back. I reached out my hand, my fingers lightly touching his, and I felt like I had touched a hot stove. I immediately sucked in a breath and bit my bottom lip. Darn those drinks because they make moments like this seem like time is slowing down. I fumbled to put the lighter into my coat pocket, and with my big bulky gloves in the way, I managed to get it in halfway.

"Yeah, not a problem," I nodded and tried to act nonchalant. I could see myself trying to toss my hair over my shoulder in an easy-breezy, confident way. Instead, I shoved my hands into my pockets as I noticed them starting to shake slightly from nervousness. *Say something flirty, for crying out loud, Lizzie.* "So, what do two strangers on a back patio talk about anyway?" I looked up at him, as I slightly stuttered over my last couple words. My nerves were kicking into overdrive. *Oh wow, Liz, what a ridiculous thing to say, you couldn't come up with anything better? Anything at all, well, you might as well walk away now before you bore him to tears.*

He chuckled as he looked down at me, and then tilting his head, he seemed to be contemplating my question. "I could tell you a really horrible joke?" His eyes were twinkling slightly as my face lit up.

"Well, please do." I took another drink of my rum, glad that my heavy gloves blocked the coldness of the ice against the glass touching my skin. *Who needs ice in this weather? Maybe this joke will warm me up.*

"Okay," he cleared his throat, "A bear walked into a bar, and says to the bartender, 'Barkeep, get me a whiskey and…a cola.' The bartender asks the bear, 'Why the big pause?' The bear shrugs and says, 'I'm not sure, I was born that way.' You've just heard my one and only bear and bar joke, and I bet you're glad it's my only one, right? My jokes get worse when I drink."

I smiled. "Oh yeah, and when you're sober? What then?"

"I guess when I'm sober, I'm not very funny either." He was beaming in a boyish way, and I couldn't help but laugh.

"I seriously doubt that," I replied, and he looked pleased. When he reached over to me, my mouth immediately went dry. His hand slowly went to my side, and I felt like time was at a standstill. I was too busy drowning in those pretty blue pools of his eyes. I followed his hand, breath bated, and exhaled slowly as I noticed him reaching for the lighter sticking out of my pocket. *Oh, that's all?*

"Hope you don't mind if I use this one more time; my cigar went out."

"Oh yeah, no problem whatsoever, it's helpful to have a friend who carries one of these things around. Never know when it will come in handy." I nodded back at him. *Way to be a conversationalist, Liz, real smooth. Maybe talking about the weather next would be a real hit.*

"So what brings you out tonight, besides wanting to listen to some hot jokes?" he asked with a sideways grin.

"A little celebration because both Jodi and I are starting new jobs this week. I am, Lizzie, by the way." I paused to take a sip of my celebratory drink. Mindful of how my lips gently grabbed the straw, I dared to peek up at him in what I hoped was an alluring gaze. "Also, I'm keeping my friend company as she grabs a cig, and the joke was pretty funny." I beamed at him.

"Ah," he replied. My heart melted a little when he smiled. I noticed the infectious crinkling of his nose, and the small lines by his delicious mouth. "Congratulations, I should be sharing this cigar with you since you have such big news." *Another smile like a ray of sunshine, holy hell, I could feel my knees starting to buckle.*

"You're keeping your friend company, and now you're back here by yourself?"

"Well, Jodi is an interesting friend, not someone you'd want to depend on if your life stood in the balance, but she brings the fun to any night out. Those nights typically involve one hell of a hangover though." I smiled sheepishly. What I didn't tell him is that the next day we usually lounge in our boyfriend-style baggy sweatpants, watching gritty crime dramas and mind-numbing reality TV.

"Thank you for the congrats. I am a little nervous to be honest, and it's a job where I have a chance to be creative, unlike my last gig, so I hope I can meet their expectations. As for being out here alone, I ran into you back here, right?" I flashed one of my toothiest winning smiles, and he chuckled.

Jodi ran up behind me, "Come on Liz, we are doing another round, and then heading out to catch a cab."

"Okay, I am coming." I turned back to him. "Will, thanks for the company, it was fun chatting with you. Enjoy your night and your cigar." He nodded as crinkles appeared around his mouth as his piercing blue eyes locked to mine. I stepped forward, silently congratulating myself on being semi-suave, when my heel caught a patch of ice, and I felt my balance go as my foot slid. As I started to crash to the cold patio floor, I felt a firm arm on my elbow steadying me. Looking at Will's grip, I noticed his strong forearm, and could see the outline of defined muscles under his open coat. He easily helped balance me as I found my feet again.

"Whoa, I got you. Are you okay? That could have been quite the fall." I turned to thank him, and started slipping again, and my hand instinctively reached out to steady myself. I grabbed anything I could, which was the top of his pants and the base of his sweater by his brown leather belt. I could feel his muscular abs under his warm sweater as I tried to unhook my death grip. Looking up I again caught those powerful eyes.

"Oh my gosh, thank you. It sure is slippery back here. I didn't mean to grab your, uh... I didn't mean to mess up your sweater." I smiled back timidly, feeling my face flush hot with embarrassment. *You can't even say belt or pants around him Liz, good god, pull yourself together woman.*

Smiling, his deep voice announced, "No worries at all, Lizzie. Be careful though, you don't want to ruin a good night." Our eyes locked as his arm steadied my elbow until I was off the ice. I could still feel the warmth of his hand on my arm long after he released me.

"Yeah exactly, um thanks again." I turned around to head back into the bar to find Jodi. I found her leaning up against the bar ordering a final round of shots.

"What took you so long out there Liz, you don't want to spend forever on the patio do you? The cute blond guy and his friends just came in. I want to see if I can get his number." Jodi downed her shot in a blink before searching her purse for a pen and paper.

"Yeah, no I don't want to spend forever on the patio. Nope, nothing exciting back there, I guess." I bit my lip with my boldfaced lie. In truth, I almost fell on a guy who luckily was quick enough to stop me from having to collect my teeth off the ground from face planting. I couldn't very well go back out and flirt with him after being such a klutz. *Plus, someone who pulls you out of thin air, saving you from total ice annihilation, is out of your league. You don't date the Clark Kent types, or more accurately they don't date you. Thankfully you don't ever have to see him again Liz, so let it go.*

CHAPTER 2

The next day I ran out of our apartment to grab a quick cup of joe at Starbucks before heading to my new job downtown. Lucky for me, my hangover was manageable.

I had often walked by the welcoming glass doors, but had entered only once before for my interview. Walking in for a second time, I wanted to pinch myself. I had somehow managed to land a dream job at one of the top advertising agencies in Chicago. I couldn't believe I had finally made it to the big time, to the show, to the real deal.

Toiling away at different marketing internships and small-time creative teams at various newspaper outlets had finally led to this. I had learned about the job because one of my friends was a CPA, and Burke and Bradley was one of their clients. When she found out about the copywriter opening, she managed to slip in a good word for me, which led to my interview.

Finally walking into the massive building as an actual employee left me giddy, and I could hardly contain myself. The place reeked of creativity, and was very modern with its shiny warehouse flooring and reception desk that resembled something from the future. I approached the receptionist with what I hoped was a confident stride.

I cleared my throat. "Hello. I am Lizzie Cameron, and today is my first day as the new copywriter." The cute blond receptionist, whose red lips matched her desk, smiled sweetly and looked up at me, I did a double take as I looked at her. She had that classic hourglass figure, completely different than my own lanky form. I grew up with the nickname "stick," because I was thin and flat in most areas, which made finding flattering clothes a bit difficult. However, this receptionist did not have such problems. With such a bold face, she could have walked right out of an Andy Warhol pop art picture of Marilyn Monroe. This girl was a stunner.

"Welcome to Burke and Bradley, Lizzie…Cameron, right? You can call me Blondie. I'll show you your cube. There's a staff meeting at nine, so you have a little time to settle in. I can give you a quick tour first." She chirped at me, and I wondered if the nickname came from her uncanny resemblance to a comic blond bombshell, or if she was graced with the name at birth. She started going into the history of the agency, talking a mile a minute in a highly caffeinated way, like a bobble head on the dashboard of an old '90s Toyota Supra. As I followed Blondie to my cube, I noticed she was dressed as creatively as the art deco floors we walked on.

"Can I get you anything, a ginger ale, water, tea?"

"Ginger ale would be nice, thank you so much." I hoped the ginger would calm down my churning insides as I nervously looked around the office. Blondie gracefully made her way around the office getting my ginger ale, looking like she had poured herself into her skin-tight, bright-blue pencil skirt. She marched me down the hall in red heels as bright as her lipstick, her polished fingernails tapping the back of the clipboard she clutched while she took me through the maze of offices.

The hallways were huge, and bled into the different workspaces and rows of desks of the open floor plan. It screamed *ad agency*, the spiral staircase was New Age with huge TV monitors playing the latest agency ads, the steel frame of the stairs curving up and around in the midst of all the chaos like a beautiful steel tree. Huge walls displayed images of the clients they branded, and the evolution of some of the most famous clients. To put it mildly, it was a daunting career atmosphere to enter.

I could feel my palms starting to sweat as we walked past a conference room that reminded me of a fish bowl. The long, oval chestnut table was completely encompassed with glass, so everything was visible. A group of trendy-looking young professionals were madly reviewing proofs of new concept visuals, poring over the different data points. Their chatter was a low hum of energy buzzing throughout the room and out into the corridor.

A few people in suits and thick-framed hipster glasses were sitting in cubes outside the conference room. They were listening contentedly as their voices passionately melted one over the other. They started to quiet down as we walked past, as if they were waiting for a presenter or manager to enter the room to kick off a meeting. A man who appeared as a blur of grey out of the corner of my eye strode purposefully past us into the room where all the creative types eagerly waited. I only saw his back, but he was all shoulders and angles, and his smartly cut suit displayed defined muscles and an imposing physique. I felt my mouth instantly go dry, and I tried to discretely wipe my palms on the sides of my skirt. I asked Blondie about the man who was leading the meeting.

Blondie said over her shoulder, "He's William Duke, VP of New Business, the department in charge of landing new clients for our account teams to work. He occasionally works directly with our staff, and you will probably have a chance to meet him at some point."

Translation: He was their rainmaker, the man who reeled in the big fish, their man about town, their closer, their secret weapon, their schmoozer, their James Bond, their maverick— this was their golden boy.

As Blondie hurried me along the corridor, I stole another glance back to see if I could see Golden Boy's face. What I saw made me drop my ginger ale, leading to a crashing of tin as the can hit the floor, spilling the carbonated liquid on my freshly cleaned heels. All heads in the fish bowl turned towards me, and I froze like a gazelle caught by the gaze of a lion.

I scrambled to pick up the dropped can, which was now dangerously rolling down the corridor close to the conference room glass door, leaving a trail of sticky sweetness behind it. I crouched down, about to grab it, when a man's hand touched my shoulder. My eyes closed tightly with dread. *Shoot, caught in the act.*

Slowly I stood up from my crouch, looking sheepish, and found myself face to face with the same boyish good looks from the bar last night, his pale eyes staring at me. It was Will—Clark Kent himself, the guy with the joke, the very man who could masquerade during the day in a business suit, and become the man of steel at night, and he was now standing before me.

He was a mosaic of class and style, in his expensive tailored grey suit, with a white pocket handkerchief, a darker grey tie, and crisp white shirt underneath. The light grey suit made his ocean blue eyes piercing and slightly unsettling, which held my gaze as if nothing else existed in the room. I was dumbly staring at him, mouth slightly agape and dry from the lack of ginger ale and intensified nerves. He handed me the runaway can with a slightly bemused and puzzled look.

"Uh, thank you. My apologies for interrupting your meeting, I made a bit of mess. I will grab some paper towels to clean it all up. I'm so sorry," I stammered, and had to consciously tell myself to pull my eyes away from his vibrant stare. I mustered the strength to break the trance, and booked it down the hall after Blondie.

Oh my gosh, William was Will, Will was William, the guy I thought I would never see again, and who I shared a lighter with the other night, and who caught me from falling on my ass—he was my new company's VP of New Business. Wonderful, Liz, super.

Nothing like making a great first impression. The new girl also is a klutz who ruins a perfectly good and expensive ad agency's freshly polished floors. I might as well put "loser" on my forehead, and wear a dunce cap around the office. Perhaps I wouldn't run into him again. The office was huge, with multiple stories, and I was brand new, so if he needs help from anyone, it certainly wouldn't be me. *It is going to be fine Liz, just fine.* I tapped Blondie on the shoulder; she hadn't noticed my clumsy mishap, and she was on her way to the next spot on the tour, sharing information as if nothing had happened.

"Um, Blondie, I'm afraid I spilled my ginger ale. Are there paper towels in the kitchen I can grab?" I winced with the sheer embarrassment of the whole situation.

"Oh gosh, don't worry about it. I will have facilities get it cleaned up. Come on Lizzie, I can take you to your desk."

As I walked the corridor, I noticed numerous plaques and awards on the wall for new business, best customer service and retention, and most creative and dynamic campaign. Several had William Duke as the recipient, some dating back to when I was just graduating college, which means he had a couple years on me. However, he appeared to be the youngest executive in the office—which made me think he had to be in his early to mid-thirties, but extremely well accomplished for his age.

Blondie led me to a modern white kidney-bean-shaped desk, and told me to make it my own. She introduced me to Dustin, a balding trendsetter with an easy smile. Our desks faced each other in the corner of one of the long hallways. My desk space was discreetly located away from the rest of the floor, which suited me fine. As I got a glimpse of my surroundings, I discovered Dustin was a bit of a goofball, with every nick-knack trinket known to mankind on his cluttered desk. He was friendly and easy to talk to, and being on the same account team, he promised to show me the ropes. I was looking forward to becoming fast friends with him.

When Dustin took over showing me around, we hit the kitchen, office supplies closet, and he animatedly told me which teams to make sure I avoided. The complicated nature of office politics never ceased to amaze me, and the advertising world was obviously no exception. While he was showing me how to use their single-cup, super expensive-looking espresso machine in the posh break room, we were joined by a twenty-something female wearing boyish black dress pants and spiked black heels. Her long black hair hung loosely down to her waist, looking like Cher fresh off of her Gypsy tour, and she was sporting bold fifties' thick black-rimmed glasses.

"Cat, come over and meet our newest team member. I am giving her the lowdown on what to expect around this place," Dustin said in his easy manor. I sucked in my breath; typically my experience working with females at my previous ad jobs was that they could be ruthless and try to take you down at the knees whenever they possibly could. It was a dog-eat-dog world out there in the business world for the ladies, and I knew how catty they could be. From an early age, I always got along better with the male persuasion.

"Pleasure to meet you," I stammered, and tried to put on what I hoped was a winning smile.

"Likewise, lady, look you stick with Dust and me, and we won't steer you wrong. Glad to have you on the team. Also, if you're looking for a good time, I spin at the Falcon Saturday nights. You should come out with us sometime; I could introduce you to my main squeeze, Becca." With a sigh of a relief, I realized (and continued to realize as time progressed), I had lucked out with one cool team. Cat seemed like one of the guys, with a girlfriend to boot, which worked fine with me because it meant less drama.

As the three of us were getting to know one another, Blondie came running by the break room, obviously excited by some big news. Running for her was more like a graceful wiggle because her pencil skirt left little room for leg movement. I was surprised she didn't topple right over as she skidded to a halt in her fiery heels.

"Mr. Duke needs everyone in the main conference room on the Summit Level in fifteen minutes because he has *exciting news*." She could hardly contain her glee, and whisked off, her designer perfume trailing after her, her tomato red belt disappearing in the distance as she spread the word around the department. Cat took a hand to her long black mane, and nervously threw a few extra strands over her shoulder as she looked at Dustin, who raised his eyebrows in a shared understanding.

"What, does this typically happen? I thought Will, I mean Mr. Duke, was in charge of new business? Why would he want to meet with the whole advertising group?" Slightly puzzled, I preferred not to run into him again. I could feel my face growing hot at the memory of almost biting the dust on the bar patio, and now spilling sticky ale all down the hallway in front of Superman. Dustin rubbed the back of his neck.

"I don't know, but this has never happened before, not in all the years I have been here. Better bring your "A" game to this meeting though, Mr. Duke is no joke—and I wouldn't call him Will if I were you. I don't think I have ever heard anyone call him Will. Even Blondie calls him Mr. Duke, and she helps his personal assistant with all of his bookings, and is grandfathered into this place. Burke and Bradley would probably shut down without her, and I don't think anyone else would want to deal with all the head cases around here. I would call him Mr. Duke if I were you, or Sir, like the rest of us peasants." He gave me his same cockeyed grin, "We may want to sit in the back—especially after your ginger ale shenanigans earlier." He smiled devilishly, and I punched him lightly on the shoulder.

"How could you have heard about that, Dustin, I just met you like ten minutes ago!" I could feel my palms becoming sweaty again. Have I already made a name for myself as the ginger ale ditz in the office?

"Word travels fast around here," Cat snickered, "and trust me lady, everyone heard about it. I wouldn't take it personally though; any story with Mr. Duke in it typically makes the rounds. Everyone here either wants to be him, beat him, or be with him. He is our resident superstar." She tipped her thick glasses back up her nose with a smile.

What did I get myself into?

"I have been told I can be a bit of a klutz sometimes, wonderful everyone in the office *knows*. Glad we got that sorted right away. Agreed, we maybe should sit near the back. Knowing my luck, I will knock someone's water over on their laptop or spill someone's energy drink in their lap."

Cat led the way, and we all clamored to the elevators and large spiral open staircases to make it to the thirteenth floor, otherwise known as the Summit Level. I rolled my eyes because the elevator button did not say thirteen. I was told it listed the floor as "SL" for Summit Level. *Yikes, and I thought only hotels were superstitious.* Cat further explained that the Summit Level had only executive offices, and the most elaborate and striking conference rooms to impress outside visitors or new business clients. The staff typically used conference rooms on all of the twelve other floors, which was another reason why going to the thirteenth was out of the norm, and therefore adding to the suspense of the mysterious meeting.

The room was simply amazing, floor-to-ceiling windows with a tremendous view of the other skyscrapers around the city. Half the floor felt like it was dedicated to this room. A huge oval mahogany conference table had all of the latest gadgets, computer plug-ins, mini screens, built-in cup holders, and wrist protectors. Several smaller side conference tables also surrounded the main table. We chose a seat near the edge of the room. Once the whole team started filing in, Cat shoved her frosty white fingernails into the pockets of her slouchy dress pants, and started giving me the down low on who was who in the office.

Big wigs from our account management team were there, the strategic planning department, media planning, the creative team (which included our copywriting group, as well as a few others), and the whole creative services and production group, which included our TV production team. I thought we would bust through the rafters because so many people were piled into the room, but with a cathedral ceiling and impressive use of space, we all managed to fit in with only a few people standing along the walls.

The lights dimmed, the excited chatter in the room stopped, and four huge screens dropped down from the ceiling. Powerful music started blasting through the speakers, and images of Milan popped on the screen. A voice-over, reminding me of Morgan Freeman, started putting the pictures into context.

"Milan; A city at the heart of fashion and design (dazzling runway images hit the screen, blended in with the cityscape of Italy as the voice-over continued), art and culture culminating in trends that encompass the globe. One new idea, one new product, brought to the world with powerful images and script, could change the present consumer environment.

"We have a chance to make history. If you are chosen, you will be the one to help create what will be a new wrinkle in the fabric of time. We have a chance to take a new client, and blaze a trail for generations to come. (A picture of watches filled the screen.) What makes this watch special, what would make this watch desirable?

"What would it take to launch a worldwide advertising campaign casting this watch in the spotlight, and forever impacting market consciousness? You decide."

The music faded, the lights came back on, and the room was dead silent. I found the visual imagery, along with the voice-over, creative and inspiring, in fact I wished I were on a plane to Milan that second. Yet being new to the office, I was not quite sure what the implication was for me—and the others in the room.

William Duke strode in, filling the room with his presence. It was impossible to miss the tall, gorgeous man full of imposing angles and muscles, with perfect facial symmetry and a stern gaze, confidently strolling about the room.

I watched the faces of the other females with amusement as they watched him walk about the room, wetting their lips, and gazing at him seductively. It was easy to tell every female in the room wanted to be on this guy like jam on toast. The guys were in awe of him, and the women futzed with their hair, and smiled sweetly at him as he walked by. It was a sight to behold, like witnessing an episode of the Discovery Channel featuring females in heat. Did he get this type of reception everywhere he went, or was this part of the culture at Burke and Bradley, as they idolized their very own in-house celebrity? Dustin had told me stories about Mr. Duke fraternizing with an A-list celebrity crowd—big names in entertainment and design such as you would find at a fashion show or Hollywood event.

Mr. Duke, finally satisfied he had everyone's unwavering attention, stood in the middle of the room, with his hands casually in the pockets of his tailored grey suit. He scanned the eager faces in the crowd, smiling here and there at some, as the women tried not to visibly drool. He was simply pausing for effect now, his gaze dancing across the conference room. I couldn't help but stare at him in wonder, his perfectly groomed hair looking gelled a bit to achieve his nonchalant, sexy ruffled look. *Sigh, he is an Adonis, in the flesh. I am becoming like one of those dewy-eyed star-stuck females. This is not a boy-band concert, Liz, get your head in the game, geez.*

His voice broke my train of thought. "In case the video didn't whet your appetites, I also have folders in the lobby you can pick up on your way out. I am looking for submissions for the new launch of an up-and-coming designer out of Milan.

"Their brand of watches is called Prescott Pine Watches. Their creator was a senior vice president at Rolex before he started his own company, and he hopes to penetrate the market and gain market share internationally." I marveled as Mr. Duke strode effortlessly across the room, hands slipped in his pockets as he looked around, engaging with everyone as he spoke. People were hanging on his every word, with bated breath.

"Everything else you need to know is in the folder, such as target market, the different campaign timelines, how many mockups we need for each, and the creative vision behind the brand. We will choose one submission, and the winner will be brought in to help run point on this new exciting project, with a combined additional team of my choosing. Any other questions can be directed to my personal assistant, Max. Thank you, and good luck."

He gave a quick nod and strode out of the conference room occasionally offering a generic "Hi, how are you" as he passed; I doubt he knew their names. As soon as he left the conference area, the room erupted into hurried murmurs and movements. It seemed like everyone was in a rush to grab the folders waiting in the lobby.

"Aren't you a lucky girl, so much excitement for a first day?" Cat marveled as we walked out of the conference room.

"Yeah, lucky me, but I doubt being so new I have a chance at this. I don't think I should have worn these heels the first day because they make stair climbing a bit risky. Seeing as how I already made a mess in the hallway, I might as well wait for the herds of people to return from grabbing their folders before I attempt trying to make it down there. See you guys back at our desks," I said with a wave as they got swallowed up in the crowd with the rest of the eager employees heading toward the stairs. Knowing full well my brand-new heels would not do well in a mad dash down stairs, I waited patiently in line for the next elevator.

Cat and Dustin started making their way down the thirteen levels to grab their own folder, since all the elevators were already full of eager competitors.

Once I reached our floor, I realized I was the only one walking around. Everyone else must be busy fighting each other over the paperwork. I walked past the main fish-bowl conference room where I had dropped my ginger ale earlier, and noticed the door was closed. I decided now was a good time to take a quick peek from the inside to get a better glimpse of the impressive room and view. As I turned the knob, the door swung open, and I gasped, my hand flying to my mouth to stifle a small shriek at my surprise. Right in front of me was Mr. Duke, looking equally as surprised.

"I am so sorry," I stammered, "I wanted to take a quick peek inside the conference room because I thought it was empty, and being new I am still scoping out the place. I didn't realize it was occupied, so sorry again." I fiddled with the ends of my shirt, annoyed at myself for creating yet another bizarre situation, and started to return to my desk. I had to fight the urge to run full speed away from him.

"A bit jumpy, Liz. It is Liz, right? So this was the new job you mentioned on the patio? Small world, I believe a 'welcome to the team' is in order." He called after me, his deep, rich voice stopping me in my tracks. My insides were churning. The sound of his baritone voice was like music to my ears, and his slight smile made his dark features much more alluring. I turned back around to face him, and decided, for someone with the title of VP of New Business, with the uncanny ability to make everyone run scared in his wake, he actually had very kind eyes. I tentatively let my eyes travel along the edge of his sculpted jawline to his perfectly styled thick hair. Being so close, I started to notice his smell, a heady blend of rich cologne mixed with the smell of summer by a lake. The type of fragrance you would expect an Italian super hunk to wear to a candle-lit dinner in a castle. *If I were to ever meet one, that is.*

"Thanks," I replied, trying not to get swallowed whole by his imposing stature and striking features. "Wonderful presentation by the way, I found it very inspiring. It will be an opportunity of a lifetime for whoever wins." I smiled, hoping the comment was appropriate and complimentary.

"You're trying for it, right? I am guessing you didn't try to beat the crowd to the folders, and I hope it is not because you have already taken yourself out of the running?" One of his eyebrows rose quizzically as he studied my face, waiting for a reply.

"Oh no, not at all, I plan on participating. Please don't mistake my lack of a folder for lack of ambition, I have that in spades. That being said, my ability to sprint in heels leaves a little to be desired, so I thought I would wait it out." I smiled broadly, and I shifted my weight to a more confident stance, trying to seem carefree and self-assured, hoping to hell I didn't sound like an idiot. *Pull it together Lizzie, and let's not throw in random playing card references.* He thoughtfully chewed the inside of his lip for a moment, and then chuckled.

He looked down at the files in his hand and back up at me, with a knowing smile.

"First thing you have to learn around here, Lizzie, is most people do not play fair. If I were a betting man, I would bet there are no folders left downstairs. I would imagine the others would have grabbed them all, and discarded the rest. Competitive advantage comes in many shades around here, but since you're new to all of this, I am going to give you a break. Here, take my folder. To make up for the awful joke I told you the other day, it is the least I can do. I have a few notes written in the margins, but nothing to give you an unfair advantage. I look forward to seeing your submission, Lizzie." He gave me his confident, easy smile, and I had to remind myself not to let my knees buckle.

As he handed me the folder, his cellphone began to vibrate. He looked down at it, his face pensive. Noticing I was still looking up at him, he apologized, and turned around to head down the corridor. Max, his personal assistant, appeared down the hall near the elevators. They were both making a quick exit, and as they disappeared into the elevator, I could see William putting on his sunglasses, his mouth firmly set. They must be off to another meeting outside the building, one neither of them looked excited to attend.

Max reminded me very much of a blond Adam Levine, spikey blond hair, slim, tall build, slightly muscular arms, and artistic, but for all apparent purposes, seemed organized, and very possibly gay, as a lot of gorgeous men are. *Man, that sector of society sure has the fashion trends down, and I would imagine outside of work Max does well for himself. Reminds me of the saying that all the good-looking ones are either gay or married? Does that mean Will is gay, or secretly married? Lizzie, pull yourself together, stop asking so many questions.*

CHAPTER 3

Later in the evening, Jodi and I got together to have a much-needed girls' night at our apartment to talk about our first day. Jodi was very much like a sister to me, so I couldn't wait to hear about her experience as a manager at a new store. She couldn't help but gush over her first day managing in a trendy spot in downtown Chicago.

I was busy Googling the hotshot William Duke to find everything I could about him. I found several articles and stories about his awards, as well as his impact within the advertising world, but I couldn't dig up anything on him before his professional career, which I thought was strange. It was like everything before he became a top executive at Burke and Bradley was a giant void. Maybe he had paid someone to remove any personal information before a certain point? *Maybe the Golden Boy has something to hide.*

Jodi had returned from a smoke break, but she still had the lingering scent around her, mixed in with a body spray she doused herself in after her puffs. "Lizzie, oh my gosh, I think I'm already building up my own clientele. I can't wait to take trips to New York for fashion week, to see all the latest styles, and you will have to come with me, of course. But tell me more about this Superman guy you can't stop blushing over. I can't believe you work for him, what a small world. Going to work every day for you is going to be so much fun if you get to look at his tight butt all day." She grabbed a handful of popcorn, and took a sip of her wine.

"If by fun you mean making sure I don't make a complete and utter fool of myself in front of a man who could be an actor or model, then yes, it should be loads of fun in the sun. I also don't work directly for him, Jodi. He is part of the new business department, and I'm on the copy writing staff for existing accounts and clients. He announced this crazy new competition open to all staff for this swanky new watch brand. The winner gets to pitch the portfolio to the client, and possibly go to Milan. Superman himself is running the competition though. Can you believe it? I expected not to see him for a few weeks, but I can't seem to swing a purse around the office without running into him. Did I mention I act like a fool whenever I see him? I'm the klutzy ginger-ale girl now, thanks to my mishap in the hall. As for his butt, I haven't looked, nor do I plan on looking at his probably perfectly formed behind. I have a job to do Jodi, and I can't afford distractions right now." I took a long sip of my wine. "He also said he was looking forward to my submission. Do you think he is reviewing everyone's personally? He has to have "staff" for that job, right?" I became skittish at the thought of his strong hands handling my submission, and almost choked on my wine.

"No," Jodi tossed her heavily hair sprayed blonde locks back over her shoulder, "I would imagine the Max character you told me about would be his first line of defense in this situation. I bet they will narrow it down, and they will pick the top choices. Lucky for you I brought all of the fashion magazines I had at my store to give you inspiration. We can storyboard some of the pieces from these magazines to try to get a feel for what you want to create. We have got to get *you* into that submission group." A mischievous smile spread across her face, and she clapped her hands with glee. "Also, Max sounds cute, can you introduce us?" Jodi's wheels were already turning as she fawned over the image she conjured of Max in her mind.

"I'm pretty sure he is gay, Jodi, or as least that is the buzz around the office. Speaking of dates though, I thought you already had one? Seriously, what happened to what's his face you were dating last week?" Jodi was a serial dater; there were never enough guys to satisfy her appetite.

"Crap, all the good-looking ones are gay. Who, Russell? Oh my gosh, Russell is so old news. He always asked me to bang, with no foreplay whatsoever, I just can't have that long term." She took another sip of her wine. I had to hand it to Jodi. She had more confidence than I did with men in general, and certainly was more convinced than I was that I had a chance in hell to do well with my submission for work. But throw wine and magazines into an activity, and I am game, especially if it meant I would be spared any gory details regarding Russell. She sure knew how to pick the crazies. Her dating life was like watching a "Sex in the City" marathon, but with just the sex and none of the storyline. We spent the next several hours talking about ideas and creating boards with picture inspirations.

The rest of the week was filled with long nights, countless bottles of wine, with Jodi helping whenever she could between her strenuous dating schedule. Luckily, there were no new episodes to report with Mr. Duke. He seemed to be missing in action from the office. I gathered he traveled quite a bit for the job. I was also relieved that the rest of the staff easily forgot my clumsy first few days because everyone was completely consumed by their submissions.

Nauseous, but yet optimistic that my work was not the worst thing they have ever seen, I finally took my flash drive to Max's desk. With his white sleeves rolled up, I could see tattoos up and down his arm. "Name," he asked without looking up as I handed him the drive with all of my work.

"Lizzie Cameron, not sure if I am on the list. I am a new copy writer." I said, hoping they at least had me on the list, or I would be in for another embarrassing conversation.

Without looking up, he scanned a roster sheet on his desk. "Got it, best of luck to you, Lizzie. We should have a narrowed down list in a week's time. The final four will have a chance to present their ideas to Mr. Duke and the rest of the executive team, and then Mr. Duke will make the final decision." I nodded my understanding, and headed back to my desk. Cat was slumped over with her head in her hands, finalizing a few last touches to her submission, and Dustin, in deep thought, was chewing on the end of his pencil. Everyone around the office looked exhausted. Bags under the eyes was the new look with everyone burning the midnight oil, trying to get their submissions done on time. With the deadline looming in a day, people were either breathing a little easier if they were done, or hardly breathing, if they were finishing up. It didn't take a detective to know the whole office needed some down time.

The executive team must have thought the same thing, because shortly after most of the staff had submitted all of their materials, an email announced that due to all the hard work surrounding the big competition, the company was holding a social hour at Christies. Christies was a wildly popular new restaurant and bar downtown. The big buzz was that out of the executive group, Mr. William Duke would also be making an appearance, and the invite said everyone could bring a guest, or a plus one.

I immediately called Jodi, who was thrilled to accept the invite. She promptly asked me what type of underwear would be fitting for the occasion, at which point I told her as long as she is wearing something for underwear, I didn't honestly care.

Since the party was on Friday night, everyone was allowed to leave work early to get ready for the big night. The restaurant was just the right mix of dark, with funky lanterns and light around the restaurant, and a 1920's style bar with lit bottles all the way to the ceiling. The staff dressed in Roaring Twenties' style, and they were known for their mixology and creative new drink concoctions that kept their constantly changing menu fresh and fun. The bar had some dark areas where you had to know or be known, and were "let in" by staff. The couches and chairs made it feel relaxed and yet swanky and rich, creating the right atmosphere to mingle.

Jodi and I met up with Cat and Dustin soon after we arrived. Cat was wearing white high heels with her signature stylish boy-cut dress pants, and a tight black shirt with silver jewelry. I wondered if she simply bought fifty different pairs of boy-cut pants once she found them, or if she had her own sweatshop where they made them for her on demand. Dustin wore a blazer and jeans. We decided on a round of kamikazes to calm our nerves, and Jodi downed two in succession. I made a note to myself to keep an eye on her. Usually, I like to hear about bizarre drink stories from the night, but this time, I didn't want to be part of the story.

I looked across the bar and saw William Duke walk in with a tall and lanky blond super model on his arm. He started mingling around the tables, laughing with ease, and pouring on the charm. He wore a crisp white shirt with the few top buttons open for a more casual look under his suit coat, and he looked refreshed yet poised at the same time. This was the powerful mix I came to know as Superman's signature style.

Jodi had already scoped out a possible date, and was eyeing him up from our table. He was lingering close to a group of Burke and Bradley employees, and I wondered if he knew someone from the staff, or just happened to be in the bar at the same time. With each drink she was getting a little more daring, of course tequila gimlets seemed to have that effect. The bar dimmed the lights to give it a nighttime-party feel, and some fellow employees started filling the dance floor. Jodi had managed to get on the dance floor with her new love interest, who I noticed looked dark and brooding, with an interesting neck tattoo, which was absolutely her type. With Jodi out on the floor, I was left at the table with Cat and Dustin.

Mr. Duke walked over to our table, and my heart raced. "Is everyone enjoying themselves?" After a quick note of introductions around the table, he introduced us to the stunning woman on his arm, Veronica, who was in the fashion industry. My guess would be model, or more specifically a runway model, and I immediately muttered "Ick" to myself. This of course was due to my envy of her long, perfect legs and face. I immediately tried, and promptly failed, to find a flaw with her. Is it an unwritten rule somewhere that we "normal" girls have a combined hatred for anyone in the modeling biz?

We started talking about the different accounts managed by the agency, and some of the humorous stories surrounding horrible clients. After a lot of laughter, I realized being this close to William made me very aware of his presence. He smelled of pine and cologne. *Was Superman woodworking before he came here, or how did he manage to smell so woodsy, masculine, and amazing?*

Occasionally I looked over at him, trying not to be obvious as I drank him in with my timid glances. During one of my covert looks, we made eye contact, and immediately I felt like the air around me was sucked out of the room, and I found it difficult to breathe at a normal and steady rate. I realized I was starting to shiver as less-than-professional thoughts danced through my mind. *Get your head back in the conversation, Liz.*

Jodi seemed to be making a night of it with her new guy as they continued to tear it up on the dance floor. Mr. Duke and Veronica made their way to other tables, mingling with the rest of the staff. I motioned to Jodi that we could head out whenever she was ready, and finally after a few more songs, she sauntered over.

"Aren't you having a blast, Liz? I have to make sure I introduce you to Ben, he is the best." Jodi was on cloud nine, while I was feeling it was about time to call it a night. After meeting the model, my will to party seemed to dwindle. I found myself consciously aware of Mr. Duke as he made his way around the room, circulating among the tables, being a gracious host. *Liz, you have to stop being silly. He is obviously dating a runway model, so there was absolutely no point fawning over him. He is not available, and is completely out of my league. Time to get your thoughts on something more productive.*

Finally, I was able to get Jodi to leave, but only if I agreed to allow her to bring her new boy toy, Ben, over to our place for a little after party. I wasn't thrilled about it, but it was either that, or watch Clark Kent with Miss Victoria Secret all night. *I would rather watch paint peel.*

"Good night, Dustin and Cat. Jodi and I are going to head out, and I hope you all enjoy the rest of your night." It was already midnight, and to my surprise, the guy with Jodi came over to our table and put his arm around her. He smelled of scotch and had a shit-eating grin—ahh, just the type Jodi loved.

"Ready to go, babe?" Ben cooed into Jodi's ear, as I looked on slightly repulsed by the display. I was already regretting the fact I had let her talk me into allowing him to come back to our place. I caught Mr. Duke glancing at me from the next table. *Is he looking at me, or Jodi's spectacle? Maybe he is looking past me to another group. I wonder how it would feel with his arm around me. Sigh.* When I felt the color rise in my face, I diverted my gaze. Luckily it wasn't me with some stranger draped over my shoulder in front of colleagues, and I was fairly certain only Mr. Duke caught the fact my roommate was going to bring someone home with us. I could feel my face still burning hot at the situation, as well as the thought of others noticing.

After saying our goodbyes, I grabbed what I thought was my purse, and walking through the restaurant to the exit, I felt a strong hand on my arm. Swirling around to see who stopped me, I came face to face with William Duke, his concerned eyes catching mine, "Hey, are you sure you're okay to get back?" He whispered close in my ear due to the noise of the bar.

"Oh yeah, I think we'll call a cab. We don't live very far away. Thanks for asking though, and thanks again for the night. This was really nice of the company to pull this together." I smiled, "Certainly has been an exciting couple of weeks!" I said, standing on tiptoes to make sure he could hear me over the roar. People leaving bustled past us on each side, but the place was still packed.

"Glad you had a good time. It might be a long wait for a cab right now, I think a concert is at the stadium tonight, which means a lot of the drunk bar crowd will be trying to make it home. I have a town car here you can use instead." His baritone voice echoed in my ear.

"Oh no, that won't be necessary," I stammered, taken aback by the nice offer.

"It is really no trouble at all, let my driver take you. He is getting paid for the whole night, and you won't have to wait.

In fact you will get home safely much faster. I insist." He flashed me his award-winning smile. *I wonder if those lips are as soft as they look. How can a guy as masculine as Clark Kent have such soft lips, and yet such a hard body?*

Staring at him for a moment, I was struck by the features of his eyes for they seemed to look right through me in the dim light of the bar. "Wow, the offer is really very generous of you. Okay, I guess it would make things a lot easier, and would be perfect if you're sure it is fine. I truly appreciate it." He walked us out. Jodi was starting to get a tired look around her eyes that hits her after she has reached her drinking limit, and her new friend, Ben, looked even more like a bruiser out in the glowing lights of the streetlamps.

Mr. Duke confidently strode to the end of the street, whistled with his fingers, and raised a hand as a black-tinted town car drove up to the sidewalk. A driver with a black suit, and classically stereotypical black-brimmed hat, got out to open our car doors. I let Jodi slide in first, with Ben going in after her. Mr. Duke's hand was resting at the top of the door holding it open, my hand brushed his as I stepped into the vehicle. Sitting in the comfy leather seats, I looked up at him through the open car door. His gaze met mine as he said, "Have a safe night, Liz," and with a smile he shut the door.

The ride home was obnoxious. Ben was still flirting with Jodi, making me wonder how old I have to be to avoid nights like this. Ben struck me as someone who made a habit of going home with girls from a late-night bar scene, and from his rough comments in the cab, he lacked tact and charm, but I didn't want to impede on Jodi's choice of "flavor of the week." I noticed he had a flaming skull tattoo on the back of his neck, which stood out even in the dark of the town car.

Classy choice for a classy guy. Just get home, and you can lock yourself in your room, Liz. Jodi will owe me one for this. I loved the girl like a sister, but she has never been one to make smart choices about the men in her life.

Luckily since we lived close to the bar, we made it back to our place in a little under ten minutes. Jodi and Ben stumbled into our townhouse, Ben pulling Jodi along with him to the door. I noticed the driver waited until we were safely inside before driving away. I changed into my comfy tank top and yoga pants and went to the kitchen to make a quick snack. I was trying to avoid interrupting Jodi and Ben, so I was careful to quietly make my snack and was about to tiptoe back to my room unnoticed. As I turned the corner towards my room I noticed Jodi was laid out on the couch, obviously passed out, with Ben straddling her, and starting to take her clothes off.

I rushed over, demanding, "Ben, what are you doing? She is not coherent, she passed out, and like a creep, you're taking off her clothes. It's time you got off of her and left."

He slurred back, "Nah, she is fine, she is just resting. I am getting her more comfortable." He went back to undoing her outfit and unhooking his belt. I tried to ignore how shaky I felt, thankful that my few cocktails were giving me enough liquid courage to not let this drop.

"I think you have done enough Ben, time to go, come on!" I grabbed his arm and tried to pull him off my disoriented friend, and he threw his arm up to shrug me off, but I pulled back.

"Your friend wants it, she told me, now get off me, bitch." He shoved me, probably harder than he anticipated, being a drunk male, but either way, the mere force of his shove sent me flying backwards. I heard a sickening crack as the back of my skull met the cold edge of our glass coffee table, and I tumbled to the ground.

A few moments were blurry as I regained my bearings. I wasn't sure for how long I laid on the floor. My head was pounding, and now Ben was frantically looking at me.

"I didn't do anything, you came at me, and I didn't touch you!" Through the fog and haze in my mind, I thought I heard a pounding, which I deducted was either my throbbing head or someone at the door. My blurry gazed was trying to regain focus, I noticed our beautiful glass coffee table had a large crack in the edge from where my head connected.

"Oh shit, oh shit, someone's at the door." Ben huffed.

He was pacing now, and although I was groggy, I wondered why Ben was choosing this moment to suddenly care. I lifted myself slowly with the aid of the coffee table, glad it held my weight as I pulled myself up, and shuffled slowly to the door. Blinding pain radiated from my temples as I looked through the keyhole. Time seemed to suddenly stand still, and my heart started pounding in my ears because, standing in my apartment hallway was the one and only Mr. Duke.

CHAPTER 4

Slowly I opened the door. "Mr. Duke, *what are you* doing here?"

He took one look at my head, his brow furrowed and concern etched around his eyes as he gave me a sobering once over. His hand reached out and gently touched the side of my face, and I almost fainted as my body inwardly reacted to his light touch. "Liz, what happened? You're bleeding...."

"What?" I stepped back as Mr. Duke pushed in, my hand rising to my temple, I could feel warm liquid, and looking at my bare shoulder I could see blood had already dripped down on my black tank and arm. *Hitting our coffee table must have been more damaging than I originally thought.*

Immediately queasy at the sight of blood, I could feel my knees starting to buckle, "Oh shit," I mumbled wearily, wondering how to start explaining.

"This must have happened when I hit my head on the coffee table when I was trying to pull Ben off Jodi, I didn't know it was this bad. Jeez, I'm sorry." I looked at him, the gravity and ridiculousness of the situation was turning into my own sense of sheer mortification. I could tell my cheeks were getting flushed, and I wanted to crawl into a hole. Mr. Duke's mouth was agape while taking in the whole scene, and I could see in his eyes his expression changing to something dark and dangerous. His furious gaze moved quickly to Ben standing in the middle of our TV room.

Before I knew it Mr. Duke was across the room like a flash, shoving freaked-out Ben against a wall, making Ben look gangly and feeble compared to his athletic build. His gaze leveled Ben, intensity and hatred reverberating behind his tense muscles. Mr. Duke's balled fists were clenched and menacing against Ben's collar.

"You get a kick out of preying on young girls? You think you can do whatever you want? You want to take advantage of a girl who is passed out, and then rough up her roommate? Maybe you want to try that on me and see how far you get." Mr. Duke's normally caramel-smooth baritone voice came out rough and ragged, and the last words came out more like a snarl as he barked the words at Ben. Ben put his hands up in protest, saying he was just messing around.

Mr. Duke tightened his grip on Ben's collar, and when Ben mumbled something along the lines of "She was asking for it," I saw Mr. Duke pull back and hit Ben square in the face with a powerful fist. Ben went reeling backwards into the wall, banging into a picture frame, causing a crash of shattering glass and crystal shards, which sprayed down like rain in the aftermath. Mr. Duke grabbed him again by the collar, and started dragging him out of the room.

"Maybe next time when someone asks you to leave, asshole, you'll do it. Don't ever show your face around here again. Understand? Hey, look at me. Got it? If I see you back at that bar, I will take you outside and beat the shit out of you. You've been warned." Mr. Duke shoved him out into the hallway of our apartment, and Ben shuffled off, cursing and mumbling his way out to the street.

Mr. Duke straightened up his jacket as he walked back into our apartment, and locked the door behind him. He buttoned one of his cuff links that had come undone in the struggle. Turning around, he looked at me, I think I had a stunned expression on my face, or looked unsteady, because he walked over to me and guided me to a chair where I could sit down. Looking over at Jodi, I was bemused to find she miraculously slept through the whole ordeal, passed out comfortably on the couch.

He sat down across from me, "Sorry you had to witness that. I think he is the type of guy who needs a clear message. I promise I honestly don't run around hitting dudes in the face, I apologize I made an exception tonight, but what he was trying to do to your roommate...what he ended up doing to you. I couldn't let him get away with his actions. Hey, are you okay, Liz?" The tenderness in his voice brought me out of my shocked fog. He must have asked me a couple times because he was giving me his concerned look again. His intense gaze was so strong I was sure it could level an entire cityscape.

"Um...um, yeah." I stammered, "Yeah, I think I'm fine. Will, I mean Mr. Duke, sorry, oh my gosh, I am *so embarrassed*. I'm sorry you got dragged into this whole thing. I can't apologize enough for getting you into this mess. How did you find where I live, and pardon me for sounding rude, but why did you come here?" I inhaled quickly as the words rushed out, hoping my curiosity didn't make me sound ungrateful, but I just met this executive at my company, and he had never been to my place, so I was wondering what brought him to my side of town.

He gave me a cockeyed grin as he looked down at his bruised hand that had connected with Ben's face, and then looked up at me with amusement. I noticed the lines around his mouth curve, and his beautifully sculpted jaw looked angular and strong. "A creep just harassed your friend, and threw you into a table, and *you're concerned* about calling me Mr. Duke? Truly a first for me, Liz, because when I first met you, I said you can call me Will. Mr. Duke is for business associates, and I think after tonight we can agree we are a little more than that. I'm the friendly muscle you can call on when someone is harassing your roommate." His smile reached his eyes, and it was a good look for him. I wet my lips at the thought, and when he chuckled and ran his hand through his hair, I couldn't help but laugh. However, I regretted it immediately as the shooting pain radiating from my head caused me to cringe. I'd forgotten that my face had become better acquainted with our furniture a moment ago. His eyes rested near my temple where I could still feel the warm sensation of blood.

"May I?" He gestured to my head, and I nodded. He reached out and gently touched my chin, moving my head to look closer at the gash above my eye. He lightly touched my temple, and I winced. My head seemed to be screaming at me. Concerned, he pulled away immediately, "We need to get something on that cut." He headed to the kitchen, grabbing towels and rummaging through drawers, completely unfazed by the fact he was basically scrounging around in a stranger's kitchen drawers, which no one else opens.

"Do you have any first-aid supplies here?" he asked over his shoulder.

"Um yeah, I think we do in the bathroom cabinet, but I can grab them." I started to stand up, but he firmly waved me to sit down.

"No, you stay put Liz, stay seated and relax." His commanding tone brought me back down to my seat. Will rummaged around in the bathroom, and came out with supplies I didn't know we had in our apartment. Jodi was a coupon shopper, so when she found deals, she bought in bulk, and often things we may never need. In this case, it proved to be handy.

He sat down opposite me. He chewed the inside of his lip and squinted at me, "How are you feeling?" he asked tentatively as he put together a cold compress with ice and towels. He handed me the compress.

"I think I have had better days, but I'll live. I still don't understand how you came here? How did you know where I lived?" I tentatively eased the ice onto my face. I felt so odd sitting in our living room with my roommate passed out on the couch, and my guardian angel in the flesh, and dressed to the nines, sitting next to me. *Wow, what a scene. I must look like I went round for round in a boxing ring with my yoga pants and tank top spattered with blood, sitting next to a guy who could be the poster boy for an expensive suit boutique, with a drunk, passed-out girl on the couch beside us. What a room of misfits.*

He leaned back a little in his chair, pouring hydrogen peroxide onto some of the first-aid gauze. "Yeah, I bet my knocking was a bit of a shock. I knew where you lived because my driver had dropped you off earlier. I came because you left your purse at the bar. I saw it on the table when I went back inside, but the car was already gone. I know the feeling of panic when you can't find your wallet or cellphone, and I didn't want you to have to worry. Without another way to contact you, I thought I would quickly run over. Plus, you live so close so it was no trouble." He looked up at me quizzically, and leaned forward a little. "Hope it is okay I decided to drop by." Instantly I felt warm inside, caused by his boyish look while he asked if it was okay he had stopped by and saved us—it was almost too much.

I must have grabbed just one of the little bags I keep in my bag instead of my full purse by mistake. Yes, it is okay; it is more than okay. Stop by whenever you like, day or night, stay forever if you want. Marry me and have my babies. Drool.

He went on, "The timing with your visitor was just an extra surprise, I guess it was a good thing you forgot your bag." He grinned, the dark stubble on his chin accentuating his strong jawline. "Here, lean back a little." I did as I was told. My breath caught in my throat as he leaned over and gently tilted my head back.

He gazed at my face, and I realized I was holding my breath. "Doesn't look like you will need stitches, which is a good sign, but we need to make sure it heals properly so you don't scar. I spent a large part of my collegiate life playing club rugby, so

I have seen quite a few injuries in my time. This next part is going to hurt a little bit though." He raised an eyebrow, "Are you ready?"

I swallowed hard and nodded. I braced myself as he gently used the hydrogen peroxide; it took everything in me not to run around the room screaming. I hate the burning pain from cleaning any wound, and the size of the gash on my forehead magnified the feeling a hundred fold. The searing pain I experienced is what I would imagine it would feel like to be an ant getting burned under a magnifying glass in the sun. When the pain seemed to radiate all over my body, and was almost too much to bear, I bit my lip to stop myself from making a noise as I didn't want to seem like a wimp in front of Will. I know he could sense my discomfort, and he graciously tried to take my mind off the pain.

"Liz, I have a very important question for you, and I'm going to need you to think long and hard about this, okay?" he murmured as I scowled back in agreement.

"Where would you find a cow with no legs?" I could hear a hint of laughter in his voice as he tried his second round of first-class jokes on me.

"Hmm, I don't know, Will, where would you find a cow with no legs?"

"Right where you left it. I should be all done with the hydrogen peroxide now." I opened my clenched eyes and found his eyes peering into mine. I smiled sleepily, exhausted from the emotional toll of the night, and the never-ending disco beat which was my pounding head from the trauma of the evening.

The intensity of his gaze reminded me of a wolf's stare,

unflinching and unyielding. Growing up I used to save my allowance money to adopt wolves. As a kid I thought it was the coolest thing because they would send you the picture and name of your wolf, and tell you how your money was going to support the wolf. My mind went back to then for some reason. I would hang those pictures and gaze into the wolf's entrancing eyes—and Will's eyes caught me in the same way. I told myself to pull it together; he has a girlfriend, for crying out loud, I sighed at the thought.

Will moved back, "What's wrong?" Concerned, he searched my face. "Hope my joke wasn't too painful for you." He arched a brow, waiting for my response.

I took a breath, "Ha, no. I happen to like your jokes. Will, I just realized you left everyone at the party though, your driver is outside, and your girlfriend is still at the party. I kept you too long, I am so sorry. You can go back, I am fine really." I stood, and immediately felt lightheaded. He reached out to steady me. He stood up, towering over me, his hand still on my arm. It left me feeling grounded and safe with his steady hand keeping me balanced.

"There you go again, that guy could have really hurt you, and you're worried about my driver. Do you have a headache or feel nauseous at all? You're a little off balance, and with a hit like you had, you could have a concussion. Do you have a flashlight I can use?" *A flashlight, that's random.* "Um, yeah I think we do. If we had one it would be in the kitchen."

Will returned with the flashlight and stood in front of me. "Watch the flashlight, okay? I learned this trick back during my rugby days. It is an easy way to rule out a concussion, and make sure a head injury isn't serious." I followed the light. "Your pupils are constricting, which is good. It means you're responding normally to light, I think you will be fine. You sure you're going to be okay here by yourself? Your roommate is not going to be any help tonight if you need it." Jodi was still slumbering peacefully on the couch, unaware of the night's activities.

"Yeah, I am going to be fine. Thank you, for everything. Oh my gosh, Will, your hand!" His knuckles were bruised and swollen from his hand connecting with Ben's stubborn face. Before I knew what I was doing, I touched his hand to look closer, and dropped it quickly when I realized I had touched him.

"Let me get you a towel and some ice for your ride back, it is the least I can do." I grabbed the ice for him, which he wrapped around his hand. I again felt dwarfed next to his herculean physique, tall and strong, and smelling oh so good. I caught myself taking a deep breath of the pine and cologne.

"Not a big deal, Liz, I have had a lot worse." He glanced over by the fallen painting and shattered glass. "I am going to sweep up the glass before I go, I am really sorry I broke it. Was it a favorite of yours?"

As he swept up the pieces, I pulled the picture out of the wreckage. "No, I didn't like the frame. I should have bought something silver to accent the picture. Honestly, don't think twice about it. You saved us from what could have turned into a dangerous and horrific night, so any damages that are byproducts of you and your chivalry honestly don't matter."

I looked at the broken picture, and it was a piece of artwork I purchased during a trip with friends to the West Coast. It was a beautifully painted water color picture of flowers with the saying, "I dream of a love that even time will lie down and be still for.'" The moment I saw it at the art fair in San Diego, it spoke to me.

Will glanced at the saying and smiled. "I like it, and I think silver would be a good choice."

I could feel my cheeks flush with shy pleasure at him liking my choice in fun art, and I awkwardly looked down at my hands as we stood by the door. Will leaned casually against the frame looking at me. His gaze alone was enough to make my hands start shaking again, aware of him standing so close. I started to think about the next week back in the office. I felt spooked at the thought. *What if he never speaks to me again after this? Worse yet, what if somehow everyone finds out about this situation at work, and I'm no longer known as the ginger ale klutz, but the girl who got into an embarrassing situation with a bruiser from a bar her roommate had brought home, forcing a key executive to mess up his hand while trying to protect our honor! The list goes on and on...*

I decided I had to say something. "Will, can we maybe not say anything about this to anyone? When I see you next, I want to make sure things are not awkward. I have to admit I feel pretty mortified. Being new at Burke and Bradley, I doubt this is how people typically make their first impressions with you, and I can't put into words how embarrassed I am about all of this. I'm truly humbled by how great you have been through this whole ordeal. Seriously, I mean you didn't have to do any of this. You're a VP, you basically are the whole new business department, which makes you our very own local celebrity, and I'm a copywriter. Typically copywriters are more invisible, I guess, I'm sorry I don't know what I am trying to say." I trailed off timidly, wringing my hands as I struggled to find the words, with my head still a fog.

He looked down at me again with his sexy, intense gaze, and a slight grin pulled the corners of his mouth up slightly. *What would he do if I were to kiss the corners of his mouth right now, down to his perfectly tanned neck, right down to his chiseled pecks, and down a little farther.* I bit my lip at this new thought. *Geez, get a couple of drinks in you Liz, and your mind goes right in the gutter.*

Hands in his pocket, his white collared shirt opened slightly so the line that runs from the collarbone between the pecs was barely visible. *Sigh, muscular perfection.*

"First of all, you have nothing to be mortified or sorry about, Liz. You forgot your bag, and I was bringing it to you, and happened to find you trying to help your friend. In the process of helping your friend you got hurt, and I stayed to make sure you were okay. Burke and Bradley is a family, and titles are just names attached to people there. No one should be invisible, and for the little time I have known you, I can tell you're certainly not. There is nothing to be awkward about, and nothing to tell, so nothing to worry about. Kind of you to inquire, but my date is with some of the executives' wives so she is fine. You did get one thing dead wrong though, Liz." I looked at him puzzled.

He took a breath, and said with his low, soothing voice, "The girl you saw me with, Veronica, well, she is not my girlfriend." He gave me a cockeyed grin.

"Oh," I replied, blushing so hard I was convinced my face would be permanently pink.

His quizzical expression made it look as if he could read my thoughts, "So are we good?"

I sucked in a breath. "Yeah, yeah we are good. Thanks again, Will, have a good night, and thanks for understanding." In the hallway, he turned back around to me once more.

He looked like he was going to interject, he had a thoughtful expression on his face, as an inner struggle waged behind his eyes. He looked down at his hands as if he was wrestling with the notion of whether or not he should say something more. Looking up he simply nodded. "Night Liz, stay safe."

I smiled and closed the door behind him. I leaned back against the door and slumped to the floor. How was I ever going to sleep tonight after all that? I could still smell him in the room, and it smelled like heaven to me.

CHAPTER 5

The next week at work I didn't see Will once. I did get a lot of questions regarding my head injury, to which I responded I was getting a box off a high shelf at my apartment, and a heavy object fell in the process. It seemed to satisfy everyone who asked, and because I had had the ginger ale kerfuffle the first day on the job, they bought the story since they assumed I must be clumsy by nature. It was still embarrassing to walk around with a shiner, especially because makeup can only do so much. I practically had to buy a whole line of products to try to cake enough makeup on my face so I could leave my apartment without looking like a Mack truck hit me.

Luckily I had enough work to keep my mind off the whole ordeal. The office turned into a quiet buzz of creativity and emotion leading up to the campaign selection process for

Prescott Pine Watches. Everyone was fighting to win the spot.

Dustin and Cat invited me to several happy hours to talk about our submissions, but to this point I had turned them down, saying I was behind on my other copy assignments. I was too nervous to talk about my pitch with anyone else. I continued to frequently mull over the ideas I submitted. I couldn't help but wonder if I made the right choices, if my submission was good enough, or if I would be laughed out of the room when they return my submission and politely tell me to look for another job. Knowing my chances were slim to none to get selected as the top four did nothing to calm my nerves. My experience with Will at my apartment made the idea of him looking over my materials much worse. I was queasy at the thought of him thinking my ideas were horrible, and I would be mortified. I had to admit, the very thought of him hating my material made me incredibly anxious at the prospect of my work hitting his desk.

I was determined to take my submission home with me again for another night of internal scrutiny when we all received an email about the submission process. In bold lettering the email read:

Due to all of the high-quality submissions, we have changed the submission process. Instead of narrowing down the submissions to the top four from the company, we will invite the top *ten* submissions to present their full proposal in front of our elite judges. This full proposal includes a six-month plan detailing how your advertising campaign will roll out, along with a proposed timeline, as if you were pitching the material to the client directly. Those from the executive team chosen as judges will be viewing the presentations at the Fox-

Worth Theatre. All submissions are due, and the announced top ten will present in one week for consideration. Good luck, and *thanks for all the hard work.*

Ah, a new wrinkle in the proposal. Someone behind me cleared his throat. I jumped a mile and gasped, turning around to see an amused Max, Will's assistant, staring at me. "Jumpy, aren't you?" He grinned at me with his tattooed arms crossed, and waited patiently as I regained my composure.

"Yeah, sorry, I was concentrating on an email about the submission process, and I startle easily. What can I do for you Max?" He was wearing a pink-and-red striped trendy collared shirt, with dark navy tailored pants and light brown wing tip leather dress shoes with a hint of reddish color near the top. He had on dark-rimmed glasses similar to ones Cat would wear. He was holding a large square package wrapped as if it was shipped to the agency. "A package arrived for you, Liz, is it?"

"Liz, Lizzie, any variation is fine." I smiled back meekly, "Thanks for dropping off the package. Can't imagine what it would be, I swear I am not trying to have personal mail delivered here." It was beyond me why on earth I would have a package delivered to work, unless I have been sleep ordering off Amazon. My cheeks were turning red, the last thing I needed was for anyone to think I was abusing my position.

"Don't worry about it, doll. Liz or Lizzie huh? Is that short for something?" He looked keenly at me. I hesitated as I contemplated my answer. I didn't like people knowing my full name, and probably the years of embarrassment from the other kids making fun of my "proper name" made me prefer the shortened version. I figured I couldn't lie, and it would be easy enough to find out in my paperwork.

"Yeah, Liz is short for Lisette. Typically no one calls me Lisette," I said as I curiously inspected the package he delivered.

"Lisette is quite an original name. Being in the world of advertising, original can be very good, but it is simply food for thought. Enjoy your package, Lisette." Max strode off toward the executive offices, dialing a number on his cell phone.

As I turned the smooth package around in my hands, my mind wandered to what Will, Mr. Duke, was doing, and why we hadn't seen him in the office since the work party. I suddenly was very envious of Max's job. The scenery Max got accustomed to, primarily Will's chiseled features and Adonis body, day in and day out, was enough to make you weep. I found myself slightly annoyed at my incessant curiosity about Will. *Liz, you don't have to know where superman is all day every day. Get over yourself.*

Turning my attention back to the package, I quickly tore in to see what it could be. I gasped as underneath tissue paper and packaging bubbles was a gorgeous silver frame with a note attached.

"Hope this is what you envisioned, a picture like yours deserves a nice frame. Also, so you don't worry, my driver didn't mind waiting for me at all the other night. I'm glad I stopped by. All the best, Will."

I think my heart literally skipped five beats. I turned the frame over in my hands. It looked very expensive and great quality. *I think this is the most beautiful frame I had ever seen.*

Best of all, it is from my guardian angel himself, Mr. William Duke. This means he was thinking of me, or at least thought of me once since the episode at my apartment.

Cat walked over, "Hey lady, nice frame. I never thought of having packages delivered here, what a great idea. I hate the thought of my packages sitting at the grungy front office of my apartment building. They are probably opening everything before I pick it up, and I swear I lose half the things I order in transit because of them. Nice frame, Liz, where did you order it from?" Cat was smacking on some gum as she picked up the frame and turned it over in her hands. Luckily I had slipped the card into my purse so she didn't see the note. In order to explain the gift, I had to quickly come up with something.

"Um, it was from my mom who shipped it here instead of my place by mistake. It is for my, um, birthday. A belated gift; my mom is so forgetful." I blushed at my own outrageous lie. I only hoped it was not too evident I'd made up a story on the spot. Cat studied my face for a moment, and shrugged.

"Gosh Liz, if we had known it was your birthday, we would have taken you out. Let's go out tonight to celebrate, come on. Dustin and I were chatting about how we have nothing going on, and you have got to come out with us. The bar down the road has great happy hour specials." Cat put her hands together, and ran her fingers together like a plotting evil doer, her voice trailed up as she eagerly awaited my response. I smiled back, realizing I probably couldn't get myself out of this one.

"Sure, great. Who am I to turn down another happy hour?" I acquiesced, and started gathering up my things from my desk for the evening. I noticed a flash of color out of the corner of my eye, and turned around to find a greasy-haired guy with a small weasel-like face wearing a look of either veiled disgust, like you taken a bit of a piece of cheese gone bad, or a grim smile. I couldn't be sure.

"Jason, we didn't see you there." Cat snarled, "Do you make a habit of lurking behind people, listening to their conversations?" She put on a sickly sweet smile, and he grimaced back.

"Cat, Cat, when are you going to learn? You have to be nicer to me around here, because I'm your ticket to fame. All of those ideas of yours are unrealized ideas, brimming with potential, you need someone who knows how to package them with a pretty little bow, and then you would be sitting on the next floor with the big boys like I am. What is this I hear of a happy hour tonight, why I would be delighted." He ran a hand through his slicked-back slimy mop, and leered at Cat, waiting for her response. She gave him a look that could melt butter.

"Very funny, Jason, and here I thought you would burst into flame if you stepped outside of your cave into sunlight. As for my ticket to success, I don't think I should be taking advice from you. If I ever catch you going through my desk again, snooping around my materials for clients, you're going to wish you never laid eyes on me. Understood?" Cat's fists were clenched, and she was talking through her teeth, I watched like a mouse in the corner as the exchange took place. I got the distinct impression there was a lot of history between those two, and I didn't want to get in the middle.

"Tisk, tisk Cat. Temper, but suit yourself. If you change

your mind, you know where to find me, by the executive's suites upstairs. Who is your new friend, I don't think I was introduced?" Taking a deep breath helped to settle my nerves as the weasel turned towards me, glaring with beady little eyes.

"I'm Liz, I'm a new copywriter with Burke and Bradley." I tried my best to look pleasant, while out of the corner of my eye I could see Dustin eyeing Cat and Jason warily from a distance. I self-consciously toyed with my thumb ring.

"Charmed, well, kids I got to run. Phil has an important assignment he wants to brief me on at the executive level. Maybe we can catch a drink together sometime, Liz, and I can teach you the ropes. Dustin and Cat will be able to show you the basics, but if you want to take it to the next level, you know where to find me. Ciao." He gave me a wink, and that creep made me feel like I needed to take a shower. Everything about him oozed bad news. Cat and Dustin's expression indicated they felt the same.

"What was all of that about?" I asked once he was safely out of earshot.

"Ugh, it was Jason. Notorious scoundrel around the office, nothing is beneath him as I'm convinced he has no soul, and therefore no morals. I caught him trying to steal some of my ideas one time as he rifled through my desk. I should have waited a couple more minutes so I could have caught him red handed taking something, but I was so angry I didn't have a chance to catch him with any hard evidence. I have heard from others that their things will randomly disappear, and next thing you know Jason will pitch a variation of their ideas—but no one can prove it. He has all the executives fooled though, especially Phil Burns. My only advice would be to avoid Jason if you can," Cat scoffed.

"Good to know, I should do happy hour with you two more often. Sounds like I have a lot more to learn about this place."

"Oh yeah, you have no idea. First round is on me, let's get out of this place and knock back a couple." Dustin led the charge down the road to a fun and lively Irish bar. Several drinks later, I was laughing so hard I was crying, and figured it was time to call it a night.

Back at the office, the days seemed to drag by until finally the top ten announcements hit our desks. A collective silence hit the floor as one employee yelled out, "check your email," which sent every employee clamoring back to their desks and laptops.

I opened the email, and held my breath as I read the list of names.

The top ten names of the candidates who will present to the panel of executive judges at the Fox-Worth Theatre are, in no particular order:

Sam Wesley, Cynthia Rowley, Cat Colburn, Jason Dean, Rachel Timmerman, Todd Peterson, Drew Hardy, Katy Thurston, Maddox Parker, and Liz Cameron.

I did not read the rest of the email, in fact, I couldn't make it past the second line. *Is that my name as part of the top ten? Can that be possible, or is there another Liz Cameron?* I checked the email directory, and found only one Liz Cameron. My mouth dropped. *I made it, and Cat also made it.* I jumped to my feet and ran over to her desk. We had a semi-quiet shrieking fit together with hugs for about five minutes. Then we realized Dustin didn't make the cut. We found him in the break room getting some more coffee.

"Hey Dust, we are really sorry you didn't make it. From what you told us at happy hour, your project sounded fantastic, so don't let it get you down." Cat said, patting him on the arm.

"No biggie, I don't think this campaign is really my scene anyway. So proud of you girls though, I will be your biggest cheerleader in the audience. We have to make sure one of you wins instead of Jason." I could see Cat's face turn a little red. We both had missed his name on the roster. I could tell it made Cat nervous to have him in the running with her, but I was convinced only good clean professional play would win this one. He couldn't actually think he would get by with a stolen idea since everyone had to submit the proposals beforehand.

I couldn't stop smiling, I was blown away that my name was on the list. I had to text Jodi right away. *Jodi, you won't believe it, I made the top 10!! Yay, let's crack open a new bottle of wine tonight! Thanks for all the support! – Liz*

I waited a couple seconds for my familiar ping from my phone. *You go girl! Does that mean Superman will be judging? How hot. – Jodi*

I almost dropped my phone. *Crap, this means I will have to present in front of Will since he will undoubtedly be part of the panel of judges. Why didn't that thought occur to me before? I was too busy being self-absorbed to understand what this really means. Maybe he will be sick that day, and I won't have to do it in front of him. No, they would reschedule it. Eeek, I can't present in front of him, I will get too nervous. The mere smell of him is enough to make me pass out. Crap, I'm doomed.*

Suddenly I wasn't as excited about the honor anymore. I was too busy figuring out how I could physically get on the stage without dying of nerves. I cleared my social calendar for each day leading up to the presentation. If I had any shot in hell of not making a total and complete fool of myself, I would have to practice to the point where I could do this frontwards and back, drunk or sober, sleeping or awake. *Maybe I could take some shots before I have to get up there, yeah great idea Liz, why not become a raging alcoholic over this. Ugh, the next few days are going to be hell.*

There are people in this world that can get in front of an audience to make an important presentation, and it doesn't faze them in the least, but of course I am not one of those people. I had to make sure I was wearing clothes that wouldn't show I was sweating on stage, because I would be sweating buckets. My palms were sweaty, I could hardly eat anything with the incessant butterflies in my stomach, and whenever I sat down, my knees started knocking together. I finally realized why they had the saying, "knees are knocking," because low and behold, that actually happens to someone who is so nervous they are on the brink of an emotional breakdown. My only saving grace was the hope that the moment I hit the stage, I would go into performance mode, and the nerves would melt away. Growing up playing sports, and being in theatre, it worked. But, I also realized this could be the *first time* it didn't go away.

The day finally arrived. I sighed as I wiped my sweaty palms on the sides of my skirt. Ten nervous people were gathered at the Fox-Worth Theatre to determine if we would be the lucky one to get this amazing opportunity. All of us had our materials set up behind the stage, and were picking out seats near the front of the theatre in order to watch our peers present.

The whole building was intimidating. I walked into the theatre through heavy, ornate cathedral doors that swung open welcoming everyone into a large main hall with two white marble pillars complementing the entrance. An impressive white gold chandelier hung from the ceiling, with a grand piano by the dormant fireplace.

Walking into the main theatre, I immediately had a feeling of being dwarfed by the tall ceilings, gold balconies, and rich velvet seats. It was all decorated in a lavish, deep red and gold melody with ornate patterns, which weaved throughout the theatre. I was struck by an impressive feeling of grandeur and importance when I looked at the stage. Taking in my surroundings, I could not help but gasp, I was trying hard to keep my emotions in check, and my limbs from shaking violently.

A professional singer once said that everyone has nerves before going on stage, and this singer admitted to having them before each and every performance. The difference, was that he had learned how to hide it better each time. I clung to this motto through all of my professional speaking courses in college, theatre productions as a young child, and having to present my copywriting idea for every new professional pitch. Luckily from the presentation feedback I received, I must have learned over time how to hide my fear and nerves. Whenever I told them afterwards that I was secretly nervous, they always said, "You, nervous? No way, you hide it so well."

However, I was battling emotional turmoil as my insides wagged a savage war against my body and my thoughts. It was a heavy price to pay. Consciously aware of my hand's visible shake, I hid them. I was living off caffeine, with the extra shots of espresso and pure adrenaline, as every sense was alert and waiting.

I knew the moment I took the stage I had to make a fast first impression, one which resonated with the executives, for those first crucial moments set the tone for the rest of the presentation. In this particular scenario, I had no room for error, and couldn't afford even a hiccup out of place if I wanted this to go well. I had no idea what the others had put together, no clue what visual, timeline, or tactics they were using. I didn't know if my ideas were similar, completely new, or if I barely scrapped by to make it to the final round of ten submissions.

If I were told I only had a one-out-of-ten chance of living to the next day, I would mourn my passing without thinking twice. In this case, a one-in-ten chance of getting this opportunity made the win seem achingly within reach.

I didn't think I would make it to this point, so I couldn't help but get excited at being so close to the finish line, but I knew it was crucial to be realistic with myself. I set a goal to present the material to the best of my ability, no matter what the outcome. I thought as long as I represented myself well, and showed my passion for the opportunity, I would walk away happy. I also wanted to make sure my performance was a positive reflection of the hiring manager's decision to bring me on to the team at Burke and Bradley. I thought if nothing else, being so new to the company, this would at least make my name more recognizable among a few of the executives, which could get me better accounts and copy opportunities moving forward. I knew deep down that winning this would be a long shot. I was brand new to the company; I didn't know preferences or expectations of the executives like others might who had more experience here.

However, I was grateful to be there. If I could only take away my nerves, I had put in all the work and long hours, but I was my last big hurdle to pass. I had to get my mind to shut up, and let me do my job, and do it well. When I do manage to put aside the nerves, I can present in a way that is enjoyable to the audience. I view presenting as telling a story, and I want there to be some passion and life in the story as well, because it what makes it more captivating to watch and listen. That is the goal I will try to achieve, and what I hope I am able to deliver.

The door opened behind me, and the executives walked in to take their places at a judges' table set up near the front of the theatre. First the brassy Midge Donnelly walked down the aisle. Her red hair was pulled back in a painfully tight bun that lifted the corner of her eyes, giving her a menacing, catlike expression, and her lips were pursed tightly together in a thin line.

Phil Burns came sauntering in after her, strolling down the theatre aisle with his gelled silver white hair, and wearing his patented womanizing grin.

My eyes widened as William Duke strode in last, wearing a tailored black stripped suit, crisp white shirt with a dark tie, showing off his herculean build. His hair was swept back off his face. I almost couldn't look at his face, the stubble on his chin, the powerful aura he emanates, his confident gaze, his strong hard features; my breath skipped by just looking at him. I realized I was anxious. *What if he looks at me when he walks in, what if he doesn't look at me when he walks in? Eeek, what would any of it mean?*

Watching the three of them enter, I was mesmerized as if I was watching a parade go by, but with this parade came an overwhelming feeling of nerves and doubt. The executives scanned the group—all ten eager faces wearing their professional best.

Then I saw it. William Duke scanned the crowd, giving everyone curt nods and reassuring closed-mouth smiles. Then his eyes connected with mine, and his eyes rested on mine for a long moment, and the corners of his mouth turned up a little more. *Was that a special moment meant for me, or was my caffeine-soaked brain making something out of a passing second? Perhaps he saw me, and thought of all the trouble I have been able to get myself in since he met me, and the embarrassing fact he witnessed it all. Liz, now is not the time to let you imagination run wild, get ahold of yourself girl. It's game time!*

Phil Burns cleared his throat to address the group. "I want to thank you all for your hard work as well as the vision that brought you to this point. I want to especially thank William Duke for allowing Midge and me to be a part of this decision-making process. I have met some of you before, and for others, this is the first time we have had a chance to get acquainted. I am looking forward to the presentations today, and know we have an extremely talented staff. I have every expectation that this is going to be a challenging decision. Regardless of our decision today, think of what a great honor this is for you to have made it to this point. You should all be very proud of your accomplishments, and I look forward to hearing great things about all of your success at Burke and Bradley moving forward. This is just the beginning for all of you. Thanks for letting us partake in what I am sure will be one of the first steps in making history with this campaign."

Phil gave his patented smile again. The lines around his eyes were slightly crinkled as if he appeared to be on the cusp of a grin. He shook William's hand and patted him on the back with his other hand. He reached down and murmured something to William, who looked down and chuckled. It seems as if Phil Burns has been, and always will be, part of the "good ol' boys club." I find as a woman in business and advertising, you come across this every now and then. In fact, it is a term detailed online, and confirms everything I have encountered with these types of men. This is why they say so much of business is about personal relationships.

As everyone settled into their seats, and the presentations started, the time went by as a slow-motion blur as I waited to hear when I would be the next to present, which is the green light to get everything ready behind stage to launch the production/presentation. Then it came.

William Duke looked at his roster, and said calmly, "Next up after Jason, is Lisette." I choked on my water and erupted in a coughing fit. Cat peered at me from behind her thick glasses, and gently patted me on the back, her eyes saying it all—pull yourself together. As I composed myself, I couldn't help but wonder... *He called me Lisette... but no one knows my full name. I never tell anyone... wait a second. When Max dropped off the frame at my desk, he asked me if Lizzie was my full name. Which means he must have told William afterwards, but why would he bother to tell that to their rainmaker? It seems like a very insignificant detail to tell the VP of the New Business. Ugh, now is not the time to obsess about this Liz, get a grip on yourself, and fast.*

Collecting my things, I started to walk to the back of the theatre. Clearing my mind of the name kerfuffle, I started my inner pump-me-up speech to get focused.

Lizzie, remember what you have to say is important. Let it be the passion that shows through when you're out there—you do have something important to say. You have a message to convey, and it is not just any message. It is a feeling, a thought, a hope; it is what you have crafted as the Prescott Pine Watch Experience. No fear! It is the words, the images, the messages they are here to see. They are not here to see you, so don't get nervous; this is not about you Lizzie. This is bigger than you.

When Jason finished his presentation, they had a few follow-up questions, and then he exited the stage. He paused by me as he exited towards the back, "Good luck Lizzie, you will need it. I just knocked the executives dead out there." Jason's face lit up with his standard cocky smile as he walked by. I didn't pay attention to his pitch, but it must have gone exceptionally well for him to walk around afterwards with that shit-eating grin.

"Ha, thanks for those words of encouragement, Jason. Your humbleness is refreshing, as always," I thought trying to stay positive instead of dropping to his tactics was the best way to go, so I bit back my tongue and said, "But seriously, Jason, great stuff out there, really good job." He gave me another rotten smile as he headed back to the auditorium seats. It dawned on me; it is the people like Jason who would steal the proposal folders Mr. Duke set out for everyone when he unveiled the competition. Every bunch has a few bad apples.

Putting on my game face, I took a deep breath. This was the best version of Liz, the confident, calm, collected, well-spoken, fearless, professional, and charming Liz. Like being in play, I had a role, and I had my lines. My presentation and the music were queued up. Before I went on stage, I sprayed a fragrance in back, plus the stage manager approved my burning a scented candle. Now, without knowing it, the viewers would hopefully also get a sensory experience. I strode out to center stage with what I hoped was my most confident smile, and started talking.

CHAPTER 6

When I present I often can't recollect exactly what I said afterwards because my heady mix of nerves and fear cause me to momentarily black out my recollection—and reality. I sound fine and normal at the time, but once I was done, I couldn't recall everything.

For this presentation, I did remember hitting some of my main points with the passion I had envisioned.

"Time is what you make it...your constant companion through life.... What would time say about you? Time defines us... time is eternity in the making...it reveals all things... how time defines you is your decision...time is a statement... A watch from Prescott Pine... A Prescott watch makes a statement... Prescott is not for everyone... it is for those who are unstoppable (on the screen appears mockups of a well-

dressed man wearing a Prescott watch, driving a fast car in Europe)... *it is for those who are fearless* (a mockup of a young man and woman wearing Prescott watches while running with the bulls). *It is for those who dare to be adventurous* (a women crossing a rope bridge in Thailand), *it is for those who want to be inspired* (romantic landscape with a man and woman)... *time is eternity in the making, Prescott is with you as you become who you are meant to be... Prescott Pine, PP, is timeless* (cuts to images of watches through time, gentleman in suits in the late 1800s, at the inception of the watch by Patek Philippe, to men wearing wrist watches in military battle, all the way through time to our current James Bond era-emphasizing how PP has always represented good taste, culture, and status of the amazing people who wear it. *Prescott says something about you, who you want to be, who you are, and who you will become... and those who meet you will remember—Prescott Pine, PP, the watch says it all.*

I finished my pitch with the supporting research and materials I used to look into how we could penetrate the target market in the different geographies. If the company decided to expand beyond watches, they could easily insert whatever product it was into the slogan, and copy.

Long term, I talked through how the company could capitalize on partnering with cellphone companies to build out cell technology into a future line of watches. I also drafted a logo design, "PP," and what it could evolve into over time, if branded properly.

I took them through how the initials PP could stand for the broader feelings of one truly living life to the fullest, and all of the emotions connected to it. I had video, commercial mock-ups, visuals, research, smells for the theatre, and test research showing how my pitch rated with a few random samplings from the public. A few slides illustrated what it would look like if they moved into apparel, hats, cologne, and the like.

During the presentation, I managed not to look directly into Will's eyes, but instead I used a presentation trick to scan the auditorium just above everyone's heads. This made it look like I was engaging everyone with eye contact, and it helped with the nerves.

No way could I handle an intense gaze from the golden boy who would inevitably divert my train of thought and focus. Luckily I managed to not hurl myself off the stage by mistake, and didn't want to take any chances by derailing the flow of the presentation.

Once I was finished, and we started the question and answer period, I simply had to steal a quick peek in his direction. I noticed throughout the presentation Midge and Phil were taking down a lot of notes, but I never saw Will once touch his pen or pad of paper.

When I looked over at him, he had his elbows on the table, head resting near his clasped hands as his thumb moved over his bottom lip in thought. The edges of his mouth were turned up slightly. He was looking down at his paper, but I knew he didn't write anything the entire time I spoke. He could be looking at my proposal or some of the materials I had submitted earlier, but it left me with an uneasy, queasy feeling. Perhaps I had not met his expectations, and he didn't think my presentation was good enough to jot down anything.

When Midge asked about the financial planning for each of the international shoots, I said it could either correspond with the new launch in each of the perspective countries, or we could shoot everything in a few locations, but still capture the visual essence of the countries on the original plan.

Phil asked about the research I found, and some of the operational steps needed to carry out the plan. I gave what I hoped were well-thought-out and concise answers.

Finally Will lifted his gaze to meet squarely with mine. The hint of a smile was gone, and in its place was his professional scrutiny. This was business, and this whole competition supported his direct line of business. Choosing the right candidate to run point on the campaign could mean the difference between winning a record-breaking deal, or losing big time. Either way, this decision would be a direct reflection on him within Burke and Bradley. He had this way of leveling me with his steely gaze, and it made me feel like I was in a vacuum, as if we were the only two in the room. Everything else faded to black, and I was completely captivated by him.

Without breaking eye contact, he asked, "Why would Prescott Pine need your pitch, your vision, more than any of the others presented here today? What makes your proposal special? Some say watches are no longer needed in our society with the technology we have at our disposal. How would your creative approach combat that stance?" His poker face was unflinching, but his eyes were vibrant with life. I felt like I was sinking deeper into his stare, and behind those uncompromising eyes lingered something primal and dangerous.

"Lisette?" He called my name, and waited for my response. The use of my proper name snapped me back to reality.

"Thank you for the question, Mr. Duke." I started,

immediately realizing his question held more weight than the rest, more than any of the previous inquiries. "To answer that question, please bear with me as I highlight a few key points from the watch's history.

"The first wristwatch was actually made for a woman, the Countess Koscowicz of Hungary, by a Swiss watch manufacturer in 1868.The man who designed this marvel was named Patek Philippe. Originally it was intended as a piece of decoration, or if you like, a symbol of status. Yes, it kept time, but its main function was to act as a fashionable accessory. The watch served to give a unique look and feel to the wearer, and to ultimately leave an impression.

"With countless other devices to tell time in today's society, surprisingly we have not seen a purchasing decline in the watch industry. In fact, cultural icons have helped propel watch sales, including blockbuster movies where the main characters wear a watch, making watches synonymous with style. Also, as a promising potential partnership in the future, Prescott Pine could partner with the cellphone industry to create new and innovate cellphone watches, and become a leader in this new market.

I believe my pitch reminds the buyer why he or she really wants to buy a watch in the first place, because it is an entirely emotional purchase. It is about the statement the watch makes as it is prominently displayed on a wrist. It is reminding them about the iconic significance from those who have worn watches before, and those who will wear them in the future.

"The people of today buy a watch because watches are nostalgic, they represent what is strong and impressive in iconic films, it represents taste, it leaves an impression, and the ultimate purpose is to make a statement about the wearer. That is the essence of my pitch, which in my opinion is what makes it special."

Taking a deep breath, I tried to make a conscious effort not to fidget or do anything that would raise doubt about *my right* to be on that stage for the competition.

Will was leaning back in his chair, tapping his thumbs together as he listened to my explanation. He was careful not to give a single indication on his face or demeanor as to what he was thinking, but his poker face showed he was clearly thinking something. His head was tilted at an angle as he looked at me while weighing my response, and bit his lip for an instance as if he had just pieced together a puzzle in his mind.

Midge and Phil were whispering to each other. Phil was the first to speak, "Wonderful, thanks Lisette for the presentation. Good job. If there are no other questions, we have Dave up next, and Cat on deck." I nodded in gratitude, and thanked everyone for the time and opportunity.

Carefully I walked back to my seat in the theatre audience with the others. The rest of the day seemed to go by in slow motion. I was finally able to concentrate more on the presentations, and especially Cat's. Since she was part of my team, I was excited for her to make her pitch. It seemed like all the presentations were very different, however in a few small areas, people came to the same conclusions with their pitches. I could see why these were the final ten, some were whimsical, some were pragmatic, some were dazzling, while others were more muted. The judges chose these ten because they represented each corner of possibility; each was a new take. I had to remember to tell Dustin about that, which I was sure would make him feel a little better. They chose these final ten because they could not be more different. I couldn't imagine how they were going to narrow down the choices. Finally the day came to an end, and the executives thanked us again. They said they would deliberate, and come back with the next steps in a few days. We were all stuck playing the waiting game.

A couple days passed with no word. It was heads down at work, anxiously anticipating the news. The three executives were not around the office, so it was tough to gauge when a decision would be made. Then a new email came across to the ten participants. It was from Phil Burns.

Great job to everyone on the presentations, you made it a very tough choice. We were impressed with each and every one of you and your ideas. However, having a great proposal is only half the battle when dealing with new clients. The other part is the ability to create trusting relationships with the client, so they are more inclined to stay with the firm through the long and sometimes trying process of waiting for the results of a new ad campaign. We are going to select the top three candidates who will then travel to Tennessee to see how you build relationships with an existing client we have in the apparel and fashion industry. We are going to join their executives and some of their staff as they attend an awards show for their new line of "Western Wear," honoring them for their diverse selection of cowboy boots.

A special thanks to our runners up: Sam Wesley, Cynthia Rowley, Rachel Timmerman, Todd Peterson, Drew Hardy, Katy Thurston, and Maddox Parker for a job well done. We can't begin to express how impressed the judges were with each and every submission. The top three attending this ceremony with some of the executives, in no particular order, are Jason Dean, Cat Colburn, and Lisette Cameron.

I could not believe it. Cat and I were *in the top three*. Only the fact the weasel, Jason, would be coming along, could damper our mood.

We went out for drinks to celebrate, and Cat was excited to talk about how everything went. She adjusted her glasses animatedly, "Great job Liz. I was really into your presentation. I think you have a great shot at making it, plus we get to go to Tennessee. Make sure you bring your cross along to ward off evil Jason, and keep your undies and your work locked up." We both howled with laughter, and after a couple drinks, we called it quits because we wanted to be alert and feeling good the next day when we heard about our travel plans to Tennessee. *Sure, it's not Milan, but it is a heck of a lot closer to Milan than I was a day ago.*

CHAPTER 7

Max was making the travel arrangements for everyone, based on our calendar availability, and when we all needed to be in Tennessee. Since I was new to the team, my calendar was fairly wide open as I wasn't responsible for as many dedicated accounts like the rest of the staff. I typically would help others on whatever they needed help with in order to balance the workload, so I assumed I would be put on a flight with someone else who had more restrictions so we could rent a car together, and keep expenses down.

Cat and Jason ended up on the same early morning flight since they had commitments leading up to when we had to be in Tennessee for the ceremony. It sounded like Max and Blondie were coordinating other activities for us with the apparel team so we could do lunches and spend time with them to help the executives evaluate our ability to build relationships.

When I finally got my notice on travel, and I was on the same flight as executive Phil Burns arriving the night before. I gulped. It should be an interesting car ride from the airport to our hotel, and I hoped it would be a quick one. The stories of his womanizing and wit ran far and wide within the company, and I preferred to not get close to the gossip, as I didn't want to become the story.

Anxious about the trip, I arrived at the airport with a good hour to spare, and I didn't want to be stuck in a line that prevented me from boarding on time. I pulled out a book to read as I found a seat near the terminal. Occasionally I glanced up, expecting Phil to come sweeping in right before boarding time. Instead, I almost dropped my book as I saw "the closer" himself, William Duke, walking down the hallway to the terminal gate. He had a leather messenger bag slung over his broad shoulder, and was wearing a light red button shirt and skinny tie with a baseball hat and aviators. He looked more casual than I had ever seen him before, in fact I couldn't recall ever not seeing him without a suit. I liked the casual-yet-trendy look, and he seemed more relaxed. He saw me sitting alone, and headed towards me. It was the first time seeing him since the presentation.

"Hey Lisette," he said with his easy smile, "is this seat taken?" *Mmmm, what is that smell? I could bathe in it.*

"No, not at all, please have a seat Mr. Duke." I said, smiling back and fighting my thoughts. Sometimes looking at his face, those eyes, a girl couldn't help but grin like a fool. I was feeling bold and a little giddy at his sudden appearance, which gave me the courage to ask some additional questions.

"I didn't know we would be on the same flight." I didn't see your name on Max's itinerary; I thought I might be sharing a car with Mr. Burns."

Will dropped his bag by his seat and sat down across from me. He leaned back in his chair as he hooked his aviators to his collar, "Yeah, Max had to make some adjustments to the travel schedule. Hopefully you can tolerate my company instead," he said grinning. My stomach lurched at the idea. It was going to be a very interesting trip.

During boarding, Will's section was called first because with all of his travel miles, he got bumped to first class. He grabbed his messenger bag, and with his cap tilted he looked like one of those old movie stars. With a jovial wink, he said, "See you on the other side, Lisette." I was pleased with how my name sounded coming out of his mouth. He made it sound delicate and exotic, as opposed to stuffy and nerdy, which is how the constant teasing growing up made me feel. I switched to Lizzie in middle school, and was called Lizzie ever since. My brother still called me Lisette, but only about half the time because he knew it caused me make a face at the formal sound. When William Duke said my name though, it sounded like a boat bobbing on a calm sea; it seemed regal and decidedly different than anytime I heard it before. I decided I didn't mind the sound of my formal name coming from the lips of Superman, in fact, I almost preferred it.

Most of the flight was uneventful, with massive turbulence near the end. I was stuck between a snoring bald man and a grandmother. The turbulence made me white-knuckle the seat's armrests, and close my eyes tightly until we landed. I have always suffered from motion sickness in planes when it gets bumpy, and I end up feeling light headed and looking pale. Deplaning, I was grateful to touch land again. There was William Duke leaning against a pillar waiting for me.

Concerned, he scanned my face, "Are you feeling okay?"

I nervously brushed some of my hair around my ear. "Yeah, fine. I get a bit of motion sickness when the turbulence gets a little rough. In a little bit, I will feel fine again."

He reached into his bag and pulled out a can of ginger ale, "Here, best cure for motion sickness I know of. I got it on the flight, and didn't end up opening it."

I started to protest, and he stopped me by saying, "Go on, have it. I owe you one from our office encounter. You're going to need it anyway if you want to survive this car ride with me," he said with a mischievous smile. I laughed and gladly took the ginger ale in hopes it would help me stop the spinning.

Turns out there were more than just first-class perks with being a frequent global traveler. Will strode up to a black high-end SUV with a sunroof that was waiting for us by the door. My mouth dropped. "I didn't *know* they rented those types of vehicles."

"Yeah, tough to find but you can get them if you know where to look. This one actually doesn't come out to the public until next year. Lucky for me Max has connections, and knows where to look. Max is a strong believer in representing the company and Burke and Bradley's personal image. Along the way somewhere he landed on the notion that a Bentley says Burke and Bradley like nothing else." He flashed his charming "I'm here to save the world" smile again, and I felt myself melting.

"My sincere thanks to Max, he has great taste." Will grabbed our bags and put them in the trunk as I got used to the oversized comfy leather seats, and opened the sunroof.

As Will climbed into the driver's seat of the SUV, he searched my face. "How's the ginger ale treating you? Do you feel up to continuing? We have all the time in the world, so we don't have to leave right away. We can wait until you're feeling better." His concern was so touching, especially coming from a man who hardly knew me. This man was entwined in my life by circumstances so bizarre and out of the ordinary. He was possibly the most beautiful man I had ever laid eyes on, and he was looking at me with genuine care and concern.

I had to remind myself to breathe as I responded, "I'm feeling better, thank you for asking." I couldn't help but bite my lip as I fidgeted in my leather seat, being this close to him made it difficult to know how to act or respond. I wasn't used to being this attracted to someone, especially someone I had a professional working relationship with, and at a new company where I was lucky enough to get a job.

A renewed flitter of butterflies entered my stomach from being this close to Burke and Bradly's secret weapon, still amazed he was literally sitting next to me across the big leather console. Everything in the interior was a light-brown wood color, which added to the feeling of luxury. I leaned back and tried to relax as the ginger ale calmed my stomach.

Will drove exactly as I would expect him to—fast, yet always in command. Luckily for me he made it a smooth ride, and I occasionally stole quick glances at him as he peered out behind his dark aviators. I could smell his cologne. It is amazing how intimate a car ride can feel sitting so close to someone as the scenery whizzed by. Yes, I noticed how his muscles protruded slightly behind his soft cotton shirt, and I could only imagine what it would feel like to run my hands down his warm chest and defined abs. I licked my lips at the thought.

"I do have to ask you," I said, clearing my mind of my current train of thought. "How did you know my full name, Lisette? I told only Max, and you both have much more important things to discuss than my name, so how did you find out? Was this on some obscure HR paperwork items I had to fill out, and you happen to pull my file for the competition?" I was dying to know. His smile curled deliciously under his dark aviator glasses.

"Yes, I talked to Max about it. I wanted to know. You didn't strike me as a Liz, so I had Max find out." He turned to me, one eyebrow raised. "Hope you don't mind. I much prefer Lisette, as it seems more fitting." I could feel my face starting to get hot. *He actually wanted to know—and he had Max intentionally ask me?*

When I thought back to the mysterious call Max made as he walked away from my desk. I could hear my heart pumping in my ears. It seemed so loud maybe Superman could hear, and I took a few slow breaths to try to steady my heart rate.

"No, I don't mind," I said carefully. I turned a little more in my seat to face him. "Thank you so much for the frame, by the way, you really honestly did not have to buy one. You could have broken everything in my apartment, and I wouldn't have cared. I owe you a favor for getting that creep out of there. Thank you though, the frame is lovely." Self-consciously, I pulled a strand of my hair behind my ear, and looked down at my hands.

"If I break something, I'm going to fix it—a promise I live by. Was the style okay?"

"It was perfect, exactly what I had envisioned." I was rewarded by his full-fledged smile as he leaned back.

"Guess I should break things more often then, Lisette." Immediately butterflies hit me hard in my stomach as I realized with a giddy grin that this was turning into a pretty darn good car ride—one I'll certainly not forget anytime soon.

Even though I knew this crush was foolish, impractical, and the likelihood of anything coming from it was nil, I still couldn't help but indulge in my own emotions. There is something to be said for the unique mood shift that comes from secretly adoring someone, which is a high like I have never known, nor have ever been able to replicate in any other type of circumstance. The feeling of pure ecstasy as your secret crush smiles at you, makes you feel special, flirts with you, and gives you extra attention. It makes a grown woman want to jump up and down, and run down the street singing, it is a shot of adrenaline to the nerves, it adds an air of mystique to everyday life, and the cloud of happiness following these encounters is pure magic. Although I knew he could never feel the same way, I couldn't help but feel giddy to get this time with him. *Oh that smile, this man, it is enough to make a grown woman weep.*

CHAPTER 8

We checked into our hotel rooms, and agreed to meet in a couple hours for dinner since only the two of us had arrived early for the event. I scoured my bag for what to wear, and landed on a casual sundress I had brought for going out in the evenings, or enjoying some down time on the trip. We met in the lobby, and then walked to the restaurant down the road from the hotel.

His soft grey shirt clung nicely to every muscle and bicep, accentuating the fact for all the staring women in the lobby that the man was in shape. His jeans hung on his hips, fitting him in all the right places. The dark-rimmed glasses he wore framed his unshaven face. *He looks positively scrumptious. How am I supposed to talk shop with him looking like that? I won't be able to formulate two sentences without drooling on myself.* Taking a deep breath, I tried to get my mind in the right place.

He strolled up to me, "Ready to go?" I could barely squeak out my "yes."

At the restaurant it was obvious that other females also reacted strongly to him. He was magnetic; I could feel their eyes following him as we came into the restaurant. The hostess didn't even acknowledge my presence she was so enamored with him. To a room of women, seeing Clark Kent in the flesh was like a pacifier to a baby. Every lady devoured him with her eyes as he walked by. I could see them eyeing me enviously as he pulled out my chair at our table. I pushed the thoughts from my mind. *How other women respond to Will is none of your business or your concern, Liz. You need to stay focused.*

Once we ordered some drinks Will leaned forward. "So Lisette, tell me about yourself. Do you have any special hobbies? Husband, kids, parrots… goldfish?" He smiled, and I had to laugh.

"Nice to know that parrots and goldfish make a close second in your list. No, no husband, no kids, or at least none I know of, and certainly no parrots or goldfish. I don't have any pets, but I did have a friend growing up who had a three-legged dog, and I was always really envious of her."

"Envious of a three-legged dog?" He peered at me as he took a sip of his whiskey, his penetrating eyes flashing as the candlelight flickered on the table.

I took a quick sip of my Tanqueray and tonic. "Yes," I admitted as I thumbed the cool sides of my glass. "The dog was always so happy to see her. You would never know he was a rescue, abused when he was growing up; going through immense pain and torture that inevitably caused him to lose his leg. His little face showed so much pure joy. He finally ended up in a good home, and you would never have guessed he was abused or mistreated because he put it all behind him and was happy.

"The unadulterated love that little dog showed, the joy, and his pure spirit were remarkable. I can't imagine losing something so important, something those around you have—like a limb or sight. I think it is easy to become bitter over much less, so in many ways his take on life was better than most people I know. He was an inspiration, and so I was envious she had something so miraculous to remind her each day not to take anything for granted. She was lucky to have him in her life."

Will was listening attentively, and his eyes squinted looking into mine, his lips curled in a smile. It was as if he was sizing me up, or trying to find an answer to a question.

I cleared my throat as I could feel the color rising in my neck and cheeks. "Look at me talking your ear off. Lucky for you I have a one-story limit per dinner conversation, so what about you Mr. Duke?" *You're boring him to death Liz, cool it!*

"Lisette, I have to say..." he leaned in closer as if he was going to tell me a secret. I could smell him now being so close, a wonderful blend of woods and cologne. "You just made me envious of that little dog too." I laughed out loud at his response, and blushed as I drew my hair over one shoulder.

We continued chatting, easy banter back and forth, jumping from topic to topic, about things we liked to do and places we've visited. We each had a couple rounds of strong drinks, and I was feeling more relaxed from the easy conversation.

Joking with him, I asked, "Well, Mr. Duke, if I didn't know

better I would think you avoided your own question. We have talked about your rugby days, and where you have traveled, but not about your kids, dogs, parrots, or wife. At least give me some hobbies?"

"No, no wife or kids. I do have fish in an aquarium at my place, easier to maintain if you travel a lot. I think that's also my issue with girlfriends... they find me too difficult to maintain." He leaned back and winked. I laughed.

His face changed, the humor was gone. He leaned in and looked at me seriously, "You have a great laugh, has anyone ever told you that, Lisette? Your laugh is almost musical, like wind chimes. I don't think I have ever heard someone laugh quite like that." The way he peered down at me was so disarming, I simply had to look away.

My face also became serious. *Is he flirting with me? Stay calm, this is just him being nice.* I swallowed hard. "No, I have never been told that before," another hard swallow as I added, "it is nice of you to say." I pulled my eyes away from him again, his direct gaze searching my face causing me to fidget. Something flickered in his eyes, his regular charming grin returned, and he leaned back in his chair.

"Your presentation was fantastic, Lisette. You have a great presence when you're up there. Almost like someone turns a switch on within you, and you are able to project your passion and energy to the audience. It was really well done. Do you get nervous before getting up there and presenting?" He took a sip of his whiskey as he studied my face, seeing what he could detect from my reaction.

Do I tell him the truth or lie? Would I hurt my chances if I tell him the truth? Take a big breath, and stop over analyzing, Liz.

"I get nervous every time. I understand the best of us get nervous, but the key is to simply get better at hiding it. Thank you so much, your words really mean a lot. I know the competition is steep, but I am so thankful for this opportunity." I could feel my face turning red at his compliment. I took the easy way out, admitting a little, but answering with a humbleness I hoped he appreciated without revealing too much. We were finishing our meal, getting close to the end of the evening.

"Lisette, I am going to make a coffee run in the morning, can I pick you up anything before we head over to meet the client?"

"Coffee would be amazing, I am pretty simple. Anything strong, keep it black, anything except hazelnut. It is not an issue of preference in this case, it's just an allergy thing."

"Ah, good to know since allergies can be pretty serious." He leaned forward with curiosity, "What exactly would happen to you if you had it?"

This is so embarrassing to talk about... "If it is artificial hazelnut flavor, then I'm fine, but it if contains any nuts at all, I have been told I pass out, and then I would end up in the hospital. Worst-case scenario of course."

"More than just a little allergy thing, then huh. Wow. I will make sure to ask them to verify it does not have hazelnut. I honestly don't know a lot about allergies like that, what causes you to you faint and pass out?"

"It is typically pretty boring stuff. Are you sure you want to hear about it?"

"Only if you're comfortable talking about it, I am genuinely curious."

"Basically, what I have been told, is that for me the allergy creates a drop in blood pressure, which can cause shock, and ultimately loss of consciousness. When doctors described it to me before they said they considered my allergy a form of anaphylaxis—which is a fancy word for saying my allergies are more severe than a typical runny nose or itchy throat." I forced a smile, trying to keep the topic light. "Really not a big deal though, I am very careful with checking ingredients, and when necessary, asking at restaurants." I nervously brushed my hair behind my ear.

Will studied me carefully, as if weighing my words. "Well, Lisette, there won't be any hospital trips in Tennessee, not on my watch. I promise, you will be safe with me." When he winked, I got goose bumps.

We finished our meal, and he gave me his hand as I got up from my chair, which was such a simple gesture, and yet chivalrous. I found myself thinking that any girl would be crazy to leave a guy like this, but then again, how well did I know him? When his hand touched mine, I felt the warmth of his touch, and it seemed to radiate throughout my body like electricity. Because he stood close by, his signature scent of rugged cologne wafted towards me, and I let myself indulge in the moment by discretely breathing it in. My purse string caught on the chair, causing me to teeter, and immediately Will's hand was steadying me. "Careful," he said as I regained my balance.

I bit my lip and diverted my eyes with embarrassment. I managed to smile back, "Thank you."

In the elevator I could feel the closeness of him as our arms lightly touched. His shirt felt warm and soft, and his delicious cologne caused me to close my eyes slightly as I breathed in the alluring scent. I turned to him, smiling. "Thank you for dinner, it was really nice to get to know you a little better. Thanks again for everything, I feel like whenever I'm with you, I seem to have a lot for which to be thankful."

"The pleasure was mine. Thanks for keeping me company, Lisette." His eyes twinkled in the lights of the elevator. We were on the same floor, and he held the elevator doors open for me as we got out. We reached my room first, and his was down the hall and around the corner. We said our good-byes.

"Get some rest tonight, Lisette, tomorrow is going to be a long day. See you in the morning." He winked and I said goodnight. I had a feeling it would be tough to fall asleep after such a lovely dinner, but I was sure once I did, I was going to have sweet dreams.

CHAPTER 9

In the morning I walked down to the lobby to find Jason and Cat who were just checking in. Jason was in rare form. Hair gelled back, looking as if he could possibly own the hotel, chatting with the hotel staff as if they were best buds. His scheming eyes scanned the hotel lobby, and once he laid eyes on me, he flashed a smarmy smile, and then came over. He turned over his shoulder to give one last wave to the lady who checked him and exclaimed, "I can tell this establishment has topnotch talent, thanks again." I gave him a bemused look.

"Good morning, Liz. This hotel staff is awful, I can already tell." He said in a snarky tone. I was starting to realize that with Jason, everything on the surface was simply part of his elaborate and self-serving PR act, which unfortunately made him one of the front-runners for this weekend activity, which was about forging relationships.

"Are you ready to schmooze the client today, Liz? If so, then I have to warn you, I pride myself on my sterling reputation to get a client to love me immediately. I would hate to be in your shoes, kiddo because I take these competitions very seriously, and I'm afraid you don't stand a chance."

In response to his satisfied, wry expression, I laughed, "You certainly ooze charm, don't you, Jason."

Cat came up behind us. "You have to remember, kids, we are in the south now, and down here the ladies already have an upper hand. This is the land of Southern belles and all." She smiled back good-naturedly. I could tell she was excited to start the competition. I could see she was so talented from all of her work at the office, I honestly hoped she won over Jason. Being so new to the company, I didn't consider that I stood a chance at this point, but I was thrilled to have the experience and opportunity.

A member of the hotel staff came up to us with a tray of coffees and envelopes in her hand. "Ms. Lisette?"

I turned towards her, and she continued "Special coffee order for you Miss. A Mr. Duke gives his apologies, but he was called away to an early meeting. He also extends his apologies to Cat and Jason as he had to guess what coffee you may like this morning. He hopes it is to your liking. These envelopes are from a Mr. Max for you all. Please let me know what we can do during your stay at the hotel to make it a pleasant one." We all took our coffees, and had to chuckle at how the staff referred to Max as "Mr. Max."

The envelope contained a little piece of paper with Will's writing saying, "Hazelnut-free, enjoy. ☺ "

In the envelope was another letter from Max, and a Visa gift card. In his flawless handwriting he wrote out the expectations of the day for everyone.

Today in the morning your task is to go to our client's western apparel outfitters boutique and find an appropriate outfit to wear to the ceremony tonight. This is not a typical black-tie ceremony, this is 'Western Chic' event, and we need you to look the part. Your outfits will be paid for on these prepaid Visa gift cards. Lindy will be the associate working with you today at the store, and she will know what is best suited. Enjoy!"

Nothing but the best from Max, and we were all pleased he was insistent about these type of stylish touches. Cat scoffed because she said she brought her favorite pantsuit along, but I appreciated Max's gesture.

I know half of relating to people is about how they perceive you, and half is what you say and do. The harsh reality is when making a first impression, it is human nature to judge on overall appearance, demeanor, how one carries oneself, personal hygiene, and dress. It can even be a subconscious tendency. I have heard of people in sales who were told not to wear expensive shoes or suits when dealing with "middle-America blue collar" workers because if you come in with alligator boots and an Armani suit, those workers would not be able to relate to you. A sale is all about relationships, and perception can factor into relationship building in the early stages. Knowing this, I thought it was really smart of the company to help us pick out appropriate attire for a western apparel awards banquet. Otherwise, I would be clueless about where to start.

When we arrived at the store, we were immediately struck by the rows and rows of cowboy boots and hats. It was like walking on foreign soil, everything was completely outside of my style scope. I would have absolutely no idea of what was supposed to pair nicely together. Luckily Lindy was a godsend.

With the suggestions of Lindy and the associates, I tried on several outfits and boots. They were also keeping Cat and Jason busy with racks and racks of options. I felt like Pretty Woman on Rodeo drive, totally clueless and slightly uncomfortable with all the personal attention from the staff. Max must have paid them well in advance for their help.

I ended up selecting tall brown cowboy boots with a light grey design up the sides, made by the client we were here to see. Lindy and the staff said I looked rustic, yet elegant. I decided to take their word for it. I landed on a tan knee-length skirt, trying to be somewhat modest, and a vintage deep-blue button shirt from the Western Wear collection from Ralph Lauren. The associate helped me pair the outfit with the right jewelry so I'd have the exact amount of country chic mixed with a back-home country feel. *Their words, not mine.*

Jason insisted on black boots with spurs, because those were the only type of cowboy boots he considered legitimately country. The associates tried to talk him out of his particular choice, but he was unwavering. At one point, Cat muttered under her breath, "Pompous ass," as Jason tried convincing the associates he was "up on the trends" when it came to country attire.

Cat ended up with a deep reddish/brown leather boot. She really had her heart set on a fiery red boot, but the associate effectively talked her out it. The sales associate felt the bold red might turn off some of the more conservative individuals at the ceremony.

Once we made our purchases, and had our appropriate attire set for the evening's ceremonies, we made it back to the hotel in time to get ready.

At the happy hour before the ceremony began, everyone could mingle and meet. Will and Phil Burns were already talking to two gentlemen in cowboy hats when we arrived, and I assumed they were the clients. Will wore a fitted dark green button-down shirt with a design etched into the front, and cowboy boots—and a cowboy hat, which made my heart skip a beat. *Wowza, does he pull off country well. Giddy-up, Superman.*

When we arrived, he tipped his hat to me, and gave a quick wink. I could hardly contain myself, I grinned back widely. I wanted to mentally take a picture of him in his sexy, tight-fitting cowboy gear. I could imagine him wrangling cattle on a ranch somewhere. He oozed sex appeal; I had to force myself to take my eyes off him as he introduced us to the others.

There was John Judson Sr. and Johnny Judson Jr. who owned the western apparel company. Judson Sr., who stood next to Will, was exactly what I would have expected from an exceptionally wealthy man from Texas. His hair was greying; he had a protruding gut, and wore an obnoxiously large cowboy hat. He constantly had a cigar in one hand, and a glass of booze in the other. He spit slightly when he spoke, and his giant belly shook. At first impression, I would have pegged him as the wealthiest oil tycoon in the south, but with half the charm of a real oil tycoon. You could tell he didn't start wealthy, but was very proud of the fact he came into money through marriage, and then started his own company.

His son was equally as pompous, but since he was much younger, and a bachelor, his cockiness extended more towards the female persuasion. He bought Cat and me drinks immediately, which was very nice, and then slapped the ass of one of the waitresses as she walked by as a way of thanking her for bringing them over. I caught Will looking at me, studying my reaction as I took in these two gentlemen as he made our introductions. When he looked away from the Judsons, his façade changed, and I noticed him looking annoyed a few times at some of their off-color comments. Immediately Jason put on his charm to try to weasel his way into Judson Sr.'s good graces. They seemed to be speaking at length about his audacious spurs. Jason was the only one at the event who clanged loudly as he walked.

Finally the awards ceremony started, and we were all sitting together at a round banquet table. I was sitting next to Judson Sr., and had the pleasure of fake laughing to all of his horrendous jokes and inappropriate comments throughout dinner. Finally it came time for him to pick up his award for his latest design of western chic boots from the western apparel association. He made a lengthy speech, feeling the effects of the several cocktails he had consumed. As I sat in my chair turned towards the podium, I could feel Will's eyes on me. I had to think about my breathing so I stayed calm and collected, as butterflies stirred in the pit of my stomach when I thought of him looking over my way.

Get a grip, Liz, so he looks like a genuine cowboy—tan and hard under his form-fitting clothes. Yes, his cowboy hat fits him just right, which makes his eyes even more intense as they peer at me from under the brim of his sexy black hat. Yes, tipping his hat to me with that sly wink made my knees want to buckle, but none of that matters. We are colleagues, and this is a work function, or at least we're attending this function for the purpose of gaining a position at work. Keep yourself focused on the task at hand, Liz!

Judson Sr. stumbled back to our table with his large glass award that was designed in the shape of a boot set on a wooden pedestal with a gold plaque. When he was almost to the table, he tripped. It felt like slow motion as I watched his massive form start to fall towards the floor, his chubby hands reaching out to steady himself on anything, smashing his award on the table's edge in the process as his arms failed wildly to stop his fall. The glass award broke off the wooden base with a smash, cutting his hand in the process. Everyone at the table was immediately up, trying to help.

"Silly me, Liz, can you hold this for me?" he drawled as he handed me his broken award, and put down his cigar, which had miraculously not teetered out of his hand as he fell. He dabbed his hand with his napkin. "Only a scratch, but I might have to drop this at my hotel room just a few floors above, and clean up a bit. Liz, would you be a doll and help me carry some of this?"

He was starting to scoop up all of his awards, speech, and cigars that were smashed on the table as he dropped his award. I was not thrilled about the task, but quickly agreed for the sake of being a team player, and started to help him gather up everything he wanted to take to his room. I caught Will looking at me out of the corner of my eye, and he was not amused as he watched the fuss. He looked angry, and I wondered what could have shifted his mood so quickly, leaving him sullen and aloof.

We started walking to his hotel room, Judson Sr. half hanging on to me as he weaved in and out of the corridors, talking about nothing of importance. I was trying my best to support both of our weights on my new cowboy boots. Thankfully I wasn't wearing stilettos tonight.

Judson stopped in front of his room and turned to me, and slurred. "Liz, can you do me a favor? My hotel key is in my front pocket; I don't want to get blood on my pants. Can you reach in and grab it for me?"

My mind raced. *Are you kidding me, this drunk old man wants me to reach into his front pant leg pocket and pull out his key? Is he going to get some sort of sick thrill from this?*

Liz, you might be overreacting, maybe this is a normal request because he has blood on his hands, and does not want to ruin his pants... or the inside pocket of his pants... either way this is just a work thing. Probably nothing's strange about this, and you want to make a good impression and be helpful. Grow up Liz, do it fast and get on with it.

It helped that I had a few drinks myself. I quickly put my hand in and pulled out his key. Trying to keep the look of disgust off my face, I handed him the key. He was fumbling with it in the door, and as I held his belongings, I heard footsteps approaching behind us.

His strong gait and presence betrayed him before I saw his face; it was unmistakably Superman approaching us. Will came closer, eyeing the broken award in my hand. He came up beside us, and spoke with Judson, joking about whether or not the award would make it. Judson Sr. thanked us, and said he would see us back at the ceremony once he had a chance to grab another drink from his room and clean up.

In the hallway, Will looked at my hands, asking quietly, "You didn't cut yourself on the award, did you?"

"No, the blood on my hands is all his. Which... now that I say it out loud, it is kind of disgusting. I didn't realize I got so much of it on me." I could feel my face starting to get pale as I looked at my blood-covered hands. For some reason when I had hit my head on the table, and had blood pouring down my face, it didn't bother me nearly as much as the thought of this pudgy, drunken old man's blood on my hands. This thought left me a little queasy.

"Here, come with me. My room is down the hall, and you can get cleaned up there. Lisette, did you hear me?" Will's direct gaze and voice woke me from my trance as I was still staring blankly at my hands, sickened by my recent thought.

I followed him down the hall to his room, which was a lot more spacious than mine, and had a balcony and one heck of a view.

He turned on some lights, and started running water in the bathroom sink. "You're looking a little unwell, are you okay?" he asked as he ushered me into the bathroom.

"Yeah," I managed to say. "I am getting a little grossed out because I have that disgusting man's blood on me. It wouldn't surprise me if cigar tar runs in his blood stream, I feel like I am soaked in the smell. Sorry, Will, I don't know what's wrong with me, for some reason, even looking at my hands makes me super queasy. Thanks for letting me come in here. I don't think I could have made it back to my room covered in this stuff. I might have lost it."

He studied my face, his eyes searching mine. He guided me towards the sink in the bathroom. "Don't look, just close your eyes for a second, okay."

I looked at him quizzically. *Close my eyes?*

He chuckled, "You got to trust me, okay?" He looked down on me with a faint smile. I marveled at how he was always so calm and in control, and here I was a disheveled half-bloody mess in front of him about to be sick to her stomach, and without blinking an eye, he was promising to make it better. I closed my eyes.

He gently cupped my hands in his, and ran them under the water, gently rubbing them with soap. My heart raced because it was such a sensual feeling. His large hands touched mine as my eyes were closed tightly, the warm water causing the soap to glide effortlessly over our entwined hands. His hands were warm and tender as he gently washed mine. Part of me wanted to groan, it was like a spa hand massage, soft and gentle, but it was given to me by a tall hunk of a man who smelled so good, and was standing so close my knees wanted to buckle. I swallowed hard, and since I couldn't stop from blushing, color returned to my cheeks.

"There, good as new, Lisette." I kept my eyes shut tightly; I didn't trust myself to open them because they may betray my thoughts. He lifted my chin with his finger until my closed eyes were directed towards his. "You can open your eyes now."

I opened my eyes to a sea of blue, and his familiar chiseled face, cleanly shaven. The pure masculine smell of him, mixed with his aftershave, filled my senses. *I don't know if I ever want to wash my hands again, I don't want to lose the feeling of his hands around mine—his strong Superman hands, yum.*

Maybe it was the drinks talking, or maybe I was still high off the warm hand massage. Maybe I was still taken in with his pure smell, and our close proximity, but the first thing out of my mouth, without even thinking about it was, "Hmm, how is it possible you don't have a girlfriend?" He laughed, grabbing towels for us to dry our hands. His slight dimples showed through a little when he laughed. It was what I came to know as his real unadulterated laugh, which lit up his whole face, and the corners of his eyes crinkled. Was it possible for him to be more handsome than he already was? When he laughed like that, it could make angels weep.

His amused smile made his mouth slightly curve at the edges in a most scrumptious way, and I immediately blushed. "I am so sorry," I stammered. "My words came out the wrong way, but you seem so incredibly nice." I tried quickly to recover.

*This is the company celebrity you're talking to Lisette! Don't
make this too personal; he is an executive at your company.*

"I could say the same for you, not every girl I know would
tolerate a man like Judson Sr. with such grace. Certainly not
every girl would agree to help him carry his broken award
as he sucks on his cigar and practically falls on you as he
stumbles to his room. Your action was really going above
and beyond. We could have had banquet staff assist him, you
know."

"Well, it is all about building relationships, right? I hope he
sees me not only as someone who he can lean on every once
in a while, but someone he would want to work with. I hope
you receive such feedback from him after this whole exercise
is complete."

Will gave me an odd look as we headed towards the door.
"Lisette, speaking of exercise, we have an after-ceremony
celebration to attend at the bar down the road. I have to warn
you though, it is known for its dance floors."

We headed back to the ceremony, Will next to me the
whole way with his confident stride, all angles and muscles
under his western attire with an authentic cowboy hat to top
off the look. The ceremony was nearing the end, with groups
breaking off to attend their own after parties to celebrate the
awards, and to network with others. Judson Sr. was still away,
but Phil was animatedly talking to Judson Jr. in the corner.
Phil beckoned me over, much to Jason's chagrin. Jason leered
at me, his eyes narrowed in dark slits, as the three of them
waited for me to join their group.

Judson Jr. looked red faced and excited, "I was telling Phil
here that I have a buddy in the apparel business who has a

tattoo of a mermaid on his arm, and she has a likeness to you. How about that, whaddya say Liz? It looks like you."

"Oh really?" I began, not really sure how to respond to such an odd fact. "A mermaid tattoo that looks like me? Most interesting, and I'm flattered. What is the significance of the mermaid, do you know?" I tried to make polite conversation.

"Not sure, but I was telling Phil it was a beaut of a tattoo. What would you think if a guy got a design in your likeness? Like let's say I wanted to get a mermaid or a belly dancer on my bicep, and wanted you to pose for me. Would you?" Judson Jr. leaned back and crossed his arms, staring intently at me. He was obviously having fun with this idea, and was several cocktails deep at this point. I laughed it off good naturedly, and made some humorous reply, which sent Judson Jr. and Phil careening with laughter. I was starting to think my so-called impromptu standup act required a two-drink minimum to appreciate my attempt at humor, but it became obvious these "gents" were probably on their tenth drink.

I could sense Will coming up behind us before he actually approached our group. He put his hand lightly on my back, and easily joined the conversation with Phil and Judson. When I am in uncomfortable situations, I revert to jokes and humor. I admired how Will could talk to anyone at any time, and make it seem effortless. Judson Jr. was eyeing me uncomfortably, clearly giving me a once over, and it made me feel a little leery. I recognized the look in his eyes, I believe outside of his western apparel endeavors, the Judson son was a bit of a creep. Being able to stand next to Will as Judson Jr. devoured me with his eyes, made it a little more bearable, at least it gave me a sense of comfort.

Phil gathered everyone, and we all started walking towards the next bar to continue the celebration.

I walked up to Jason as we headed over to the bar. "Can I ask you for a favor?" I asked him against my better judgment as we walked side by side.

"A favor, well, Lizzie, I suppose that depends on the favor now, doesn't it?" He shoved his hands into his pockets as he strolled down the block.

"I was wondering if you wouldn't mind running interference with Judson Jr. for me. I have this uncomfortable feeling as the night continues, and he gets drunker, he might be the type to get a little too close for comfort. I know this whole activity is about building relationships, but I want to avoid any awkwardness. Therefore, don't worry about jumping in the conversation, or if you see him trying to sit next me to me at the bar, feel free to take the empty spot instead. I might be giving you an advantage in this competition, but I am really hoping you wouldn't mind helping me out in case he gets a little creepy." I didn't tell him about the tattoo comments, but was hoping his competitive nature would take over, and he wouldn't mind watching my back if it meant it gave him an advantage.

"Why of course, Liz, consider it covered." Jason smiled ear to ear, appearing pleased at this sudden turn of events.

We walked into the crowded bar with blasting country music. A girl in a jean mini skirt and a belly shirt was dancing on the bar top, and thumping her boots, causing all the beers to jingle. A guy strumming his guitar, and tapping his cowboy boots to the tune, provided live music from the corner area.

The bar had two levels, with more music blaring from upstairs. We all got a round of drinks, and Judson Jr. sauntered over. "Think about being my model for my tattoo, little lady?" His leaned in and slurred in my ear. I cringed at the remark, and disappointed his excess drinks didn't cause him to forget his little notion. I was looking around for Jason, thinking he would come over and join us. Then I noticed with discomfort as Judson Jr.'s hand now rested on my behind. Jason walked over, his spurs clanging. I clung to the hope he might save me from this moment.

"Judson and Liz, I hear there is some great dancing upstairs. Why don't you show Liz here how it is done in the south, Judson? Liz, you were talking my ear off earlier about how you were hoping someone would ask you to dance, so I'm sure you two would have a great time." He leered at me, eyes twinkling, betraying my trust. Instead of taking the advantage I gave him, he decided to be a real jerk and create a much-worse situation after I confided in him. *What a creep.* Of course, Judson Jr. loved the idea. He started pulling my arm towards the stairs to the second-level bar as I protested. I could see Will was busy at the bar ordering rounds of drinks for everyone, unaware of my current situation, and I knew glumly I couldn't turn down the offer since Jason had left me high and dry.

"You would break my heart, sweetheart, if you turned me down," Judson Jr. drawled in my ear. Phil was standing nearby and had heard Jason's comment, and not knowing about my wishes to avoid this type of situation, he chimed in, thinking it was a great idea.

"You only live once, Liz. Judson Jr. can show you how they party down here in the south," Phil shouted, as he lifted his beverage in agreement.

I was reluctantly pulled up the stairs to the second floor bar and a large dance floor. Judson Jr. grabbed my arm to drag me onto the dance floor, and started trying to grind his body against mine, and alternately tried to twirl me. After a couple songs, I was feeling like I had put in my time for the night.

"Thanks for the dances, I think I am going to head down and see what the others are doing," I shouted as I started to walk towards the stairs.

"No way, little lady, you can't leave yet, we haven't even gotten started!" He pulled me back roughly by my arm as a slow song started. He put his hand behind my head, and tried to pull me in towards him as the slow country song played in the background, I resisted.

"Oh come on, darling, don't you want to know how we kiss in the south?" He roughly pulled me closer, his sweaty top lip and mouth pursed, getting ready to plant a kiss. I ducked quickly, and spun away from his sweaty embrace. He grabbed my forearm and yanked, I could feel him squeezing hard as I tried to back away. The dance floor was so crowded no one would notice a girl who was trying to squirm away from unwanted advances. I jerked my arm, and he pulled harder, causing me to wince in pain as his clenched hand radiated shooting pain up my arm. I stayed focused despite my screaming arm pain, and used my other hand to grab his fingers to pry them off. Finally shaking his grip, I quickly ran towards the stairs. No one took time to notice a girl fleeing from a sweaty scoundrel on the dance floor.

Back on the main floor, I saw Will's eyes catch mine. He came towards me, "Hey, some of us are going to head back to the hotel and call it a night. You are welcome to come, or you can stay."

I looked down at the floor as I leaned in, pretending I was concentrating on hearing him above the noise, when I couldn't bear to look him in the eye for fear he would see the distress in my eyes. I responded curtly, "I will leave with you."

On the way to the hotel, I walked next to Cat who was drunk and chatting with another employee of the western apparel company. Once back at the hotel, Will and I were the only ones headed to the seventh floor, so as everyone else left the elevator, we exited our floor together. I was holding my arm gingerly; it was still smarting from the rough handling on the floor. Will paused in front of my door. "Did you have fun tonight?"

"Yeah it was great, thank you again for this tremendous opportunity. I am really grateful," I glanced up to meet his gaze for a split second, and quickly looked down again, "Have a good night." I turned to open the door with my key.

I could feel him reach out and lightly touch my elbow, "Hey, Lisette, is everything Okay? You seem a little down," I could feel my tears welling up, a curse of mine whenever I am in a fragile state, and someone shows kindness. Sometimes I have to fight not to get emotional. Still cradling my arm, I turned back toward him. I dared to look up at him, and I saw his eyes narrowed with concern as he waiting for my response. Being this near to him made my stomach lurch as eyes searched mine, trying to decipher my thoughts.

"Yeah, it's just that Judson Jr. can be a bit much. I think I am a little tired, so it got to me a little, but it is nothing really. Thank you for asking." I didn't realize I was subconsciously rubbing my arm, trying to massage out the dull ache which was a byproduct from the rough handling on the dance floor. Noticing the movement, Will looked down at my arm where a dark bruise was sticking out from my shirtsleeve.

"Jesus, Lisette, what happened to your arm?" He reached forward, and before I could stop him, he gently held my arm and slowly moved the sleeve up, revealing five deep bruises already turning black and blue. They were wrapped around my arm in the shape of fingers from Judson Jr.'s hand yanking me back on the dance floor. "Did he do this to you?" He gasped, looking into my eyes with a furious expression. I felt jittery as I looked up at him, not quite sure what to say.

"Wait for me in your room, I am going to get some ice and come back. Don't let anyone else in, okay?" he commanded, looking intently at me. I was in an emotional haze as he took the key card from me and opened my door, holding it open for me. "I'm fine really..." I began, but he shot me a disbelieving look.

"Lisette," he scolded me, not finishing the sentence, but I knew he wanted me to stop protesting. His look was determined and dark, his eyes flashing as he turned to walk away, leaving me in my room. I quickly changed into my black yoga pants and t-shirt and waited for him to return. Disgusted, I looked at my discarded outfit, and decided quickly I would donate it as soon as I got home. I didn't want anything left to remind me of the appalling Judsons. I threw my long hair quickly into a high, loose pony, letting it hit me in the back as I walked.

Will returned with ice, and opened his mouth to say something, and then thinking better of it, he closed it again.

"You can come in," I said quietly. He placed the ice on the counter, and I sat on the king-sized bed. He wrapped some ice in a towel before sitting down next to me. Some of the lights were on in the room, so the bruising was now more noticeable. I was hiding it by tightly crossing my arms.

"Can I see?" he asked quietly. When I held out my arm, he gently took it in his hand and turned it. His whole body seemed to tense. He lightly put the ice on my arm with his other hand, still holding my arm. I could smell him again sitting so close. I could see the stubble on his jaw starting to come back. He looked at me, and in the light of the room, his eyes appeared pale blue instead of the dark intense blue I saw earlier. All the thoughts in my head simply dissipated by just looking at them.

"Tell me what happened," he asked in a low voice. I sighed, knowing he wouldn't stop questioning me until I told him the truth, so I told him. Once I finished, and explained I didn't think he had intended to actually hurt my arm, Will jumped off the bed and started pacing the room.

His hands were balled into a fists, he was furiously looking at the floor, and then back at me. "I want to go over there right now and punch that scum right in the face. Maybe if I hit him right in the eye, he won't be able to look at a female the same way again. I am dropping them as a client—yes I am. They are done, they can find themselves another ad agency, and I may slap an assault charge on him." He growled as he paced the room.

I quickly got to my feet, "Will, no, please don't take this out of context. You can't drop them as a client. They bring in a ton of money for the agency; please don't disrupt anything on account of me. No assault charge or any charge is necessary; really can't we forget it and move on? I never have to see him again, right? I don't want this to change anything. Please, you have to promise me. I don't want to ever think about him again, so any other action on my part would make this into a bigger thing. I can handle myself, really. This is what I want, to move past this, and forget it. Please don't make me regret telling you because it wasn't my intent. I am a hundred percent fine. Promise me." I pleaded, standing in front of him, his chest heaving as if he was ready to jump into a gladiator arena.

He guided me back to the bed and sat me down, his hands gently resting on my shoulders. He put the ice back on my arm, and ran his hand agitatedly through his hair. He leaned forward towards me and sighed.

"Fine," he relented, "if you don't want me to do anything, I won't. I am blacklisting you from ever working on their account, you will not receive any emails from them, you will not talk to them, and you will not send them a letter in the mail. I want them completely cut off from you. Do you agree with those terms? If you won't let me do anything to them, cut them loose as a client, or go after the dirt bag Judson Jr., then I will do everything I can to make sure you don't ever come in contact with them again for your own safety. He is never going to have a chance to be anywhere near you again, understood?" He was frowning as he looked at me with such intensity and seriousness, which combined with his fresh tan from the strong Tennessee sun, made it impossible for me to anything but swallow hard and nod. I could see his whole body relax once I acquiesced.

"Okay, it is a deal," he said again and stood up. "Sorry I was a little worked up because the thought of him touching you, and grabbing you… and your arm…" he trailed off and cleared his throat. He studied his hands. It was painful to watch him so concerned for me, and frustrated by the turn of events. I tried lightening the mood.

"You know, I could really use a good joke right now, Will, do you mind?" I smiled tentatively. My question made him pause, which stopped his pacing, and I could see his shoulders relax a little. He sat down next to me, and took a deep breath.

"How do you kill a vegetarian vampire?" He leaned in close to me, a little twinkle in his eyes. My eyebrows rose at the question, and still holding the ice on my arm, I looked to the ceiling deep in thought.

"Oh boy, I think you got me there. How *do you* kill a vegetarian vampire?"

"Quite simple actually, a "steak" to the heart should do the trick," he said softly, the corner of his mouth lifting ever so slightly into a slow smile. I beamed back at him, biting my lower lip, and then chuckled.

"Good to know, and it makes sense, too." He nodded as I smiled at him. His tone seemed lighter now, but his face went back to being more serious as he lightly touched my bruised arm.

"Lisette, joking aside, it is killing me to think of him hurting you. I don't want him to have the opportunity to hurt you or anyone again. You are here because I asked you to come, so you are my responsibility." He looked pained at the thought.

"This shouldn't have happened, I feel like I failed you tonight because I wasn't able to keep you completely safe.

Although I'm promising you I won't do anything to them directly, I will however have Max discretely write reviews online to help others know what they are getting into with the Judsons. This is non-negotiable, he can't walk away without any repercussions for his actions." He cleared his throat, and seemed at a loss.

He eagerly searched my face, "Explain to me Lisette," he softly said, "how someone as good as you, as pure as you, is always getting hurt? Ever since I met you in that bar, I thought there was something very special about you. I thought I would never see you again once we parted ways that night, but I am glad I was wrong." He pushed back a strand of hair from my face. I sucked in a breath, and felt chills reverberating through my body at his slight touch. I couldn't believe he was sitting next to me, and trying to protect me, it made me wonder if I would wake from this dream.

Maybe it was the drinks, maybe it was the whole night, or maybe it was the whole crazy situation where we had met by chance, and then were thrust into each other's lives, but I felt like I was living in some sort of alternate reality. He was looking at me with such compassion and care. I could feel a tear roll down my check from all of my conflicting emotions. He brushed away the tear with the back of his hand, and lifted my chin slightly so I was looking right into his eyes. He gently pulled my face closer to his. His lips brushed mine, and then connected.

I felt immediate warmth as our lips meshed together in perfect harmony. I felt the floor drop beneath me. I was floating in the kiss, warmth spreading throughout my entire body. I kissed back. I put my hand behind his neck, and brought him closer as I let myself get taken with the all-consuming feeling of pleasure. It was like the sun warming your skin on a bright summer's day, or sinking slowly into hot springs. I felt as whole as I have ever felt, as if our lips were meant to meld together. I had chills as I hungrily asked for more with my lips eagerly seeking his. We kissed deeper. Our lips connecting were soft and warm; we melted together like butter as the warmth from our lips shot through my body all the way down to my toes. *I'm kissing Superman, William Duke, THE William Duke.* It felt so right I didn't want to stop, but I didn't have to. He pulled back from me suddenly, leaving my lips cold and confused.

He looked at me stupefied, something flashing behind his eyes. Was it fear, regret or surprise?

"Geez, Lisette," he bit his lower lip. "I am so sorry; I hope I didn't offend you. Shoot, I am sorry." He ran his hand through his hair again, looking flustered, his cheeks flushed. I think my mouth was slightly open as I was still in shock from our smoldering kiss. He jumped off the bed and paced back and forth a few times, looking at the floor and running his hand through his hair. "I think I should go, it's getting late. Again I… I didn't mean… I don't know what came over me. We work together, and I'm sure after tonight, the last thing you want is for something else to become complicated…" he trailed off looking lost in his thoughts.

I tried to lighten the mood. Finally finding my voice, I stood up, legs shaky from literally feeling like the ground was falling beneath me. "Will, let me get this straight. You're apologizing to me when you have been a gentleman the entire night, getting me ice, and offering to beat up that creep for me?" I cracked a smile, "Trust me, that kiss… is nothing to be sorry about. Really, you saved me from having to remember this day always as the day I was manhandled by that sweaty scoundrel who left bruises on my arm. Really, you have nothing to apologize for, in fact, I am glad you came over. I mean every word." I gave him a small smile, and swallowed hard, waiting for his response. His body instantly relaxed, and he smiled back at me.

"Okay, I want to make sure the next time we see each other this doesn't make things uncomfortable or awkward. That is the last thing I want. Perhaps we can chalk this up as having a couple drinks; besides it was a weird night. Can we move forward without this impacting anything between us?" He looked up at me hopefully.

"Will, as you said to me in my apartment, we have nothing to be awkward about, and nothing to talk about or tell, so nothing to worry about. I promise." I smiled back reassuringly, realizing he may feel that this was a huge mistake. *It is probably for the best that we just forget this ever happened. How would I concentrate at work if I kept thinking about that kiss—that sweet, hot, perfect kiss?*

Will nodded. "Get some sleep." He winked, and gave me a big bear hug, which left me feeling safe and warm. He was a phenomenal hugger, I felt dwarfed by his size and strength, a feeling I really loved. He left me wanting more. I walked him to the door again, and he left me with, "Sweet dreams, Lisette." Then he tipped his sexy cowboy hat, and went to his room. As I shut the door, I realized how much better my room had looked with him in it.

CHAPTER 10

The next day Cat, Jason, and I grabbed breakfast and headed to the airport. "Hope you had a great night Liz, Judson Jr. seemed pretty smitten with you." Jason sneered, as he checked his greased-back hair in the reflection of his cellphone.

"Yeah, thanks for nothing, Jason." Luckily I had packed one long-sleeve shirt, and it hid the bruising, which hopefully would help avoid any awkward questions or comments. The last thing I needed after coming to the office with a shiner from my head connecting to a coffee table was to have another incident where I come to the office bruised and battered.

"Anytime," he replied, his lips curled up in a macabre smile. "While you were off occupying the obnoxious son, I was chirping in his daddy's ear, making sure I was his favorite. I have this thing locked down, so you ladies are going to have to find another way to win this competition." He looked absolutely pleased with himself and his cunningness.

"Give me a break, Jason, just because you play dirty does not mean you're winning this thing," Cat shot back. "You're an ass and a half, and one of these times, Jason your snake-like behavior is going to bite you in the ass." He laughed in response.

Thankfully my seat was away from Jason and Cat, after having to be "on" for such a long period of time, it was nice to be by myself, and tune out everything. I listened to my iPod and rubbed my sore arm. While drinking a ginger ale from the beverage cart, my thoughts wandered to Superman.

Will and Phil had stayed back with the client to debrief, get their take on all of us, and finish other business. I hoped Will kept his promise not to mention the fiasco with Judson Jr. My chest tightened at the thought of being pulled into some sort of scandal, and wondered how he was doing with hiding his disgust with those guys in the meeting. Being so new to the company, I could only imagine what type of rumors would circulate with such news tied to my name. Once we landed, I turned my phone back on, and saw a new text. My stomach flipped when I saw it was from Will.

How is your arm doing? I didn't say anything in our meetings today, against my better judgment. I know you have been through enough, so I want to respect your wishes. Doesn't change the fact I want to ring his neck. –Will.

I sucked in a quick breath and immediately felt a little giddy from his text. My hands started to shake at the memory of our kiss. I contemplated what to type back, and decided to keep it light and casual.

Thank you for not saying anything. I will survive; long sleeves are a lifesaver. Safe travels back tomorrow. – Lisette.

Signing my name by what he calls me, even though I previously hated it, felt right since the text was for him. I felt my phone vibrate again.

See, Lisette isn't so bad is it? It fits you, and it's a beautiful name. – Will.

His message seemed playful, He was reaching out, which helped me feel less uncomfortable about what had transpired between us. However, it didn't mean I could to stop thinking about it. I quickly sent another text.

It is your fault that I'm getting used to it. But I guess it's not a bad thing. I suppose I should call you William then to be fair. ☺ – Lisette.

I smiled, happy because it felt like we were flirting with each other again. After our kiss, I thought maybe we would institute a policy of not communicating, and stay far away from each other, similar to my being blacklisted with the western apparel company and the Judsons. Wiping the thoughts out of my mind, I realized he was trying to be nice, and make sure we had no awkwardness between us.

Call me whatever you like Lisette. Be safe. See you back at the office soon. – Will.

I shivered, feeling warmth spread throughout my body at his text. My breath was coming faster, and I was riding the emotional high that came with simply hearing from him. I marveled at how one little text could change how I was feeling about everything.

CHAPTER 11

Back at the office after the trip, Cat and I were filling Dustin in on all the details. I was also finishing some new copy work for a dog-food account I was assigned to recently, and I was admittedly having a lot of fun with the research and material. However, I was anxiously waiting for any news on the big PP case. Looking up, I noticed Max's spiked blonde hair and arched eyebrow standing by my desk, his arms folded as he looked at what I was working on.

"Liz, Mr. Duke would like to see you in his office if you have a second."

"Um, yeah sure. I can go now, and take a break from this," I stammered, wondering what the impromptu meeting was about. I could see Cat looking at me from her desk, eyes wide with curiosity. "Good luck," she mouthed as I followed Max down the corridor. I had never been in Superman's office before, so I was curious to see what type of environment he hid in all day.

He stood when Max pushed open the heavy door, and held it for me as I entered. Will had on his trademark white button shirt with several of the top buttons opened for a casual look. The shirt must be linen or some sort of light material because I could see a glimpse of his tanned body underneath. He wore a light-brown edgy sports jacket with the sleeves rolled up, and the collar slightly up in the back. His brown hair looking messy and casually styled, like he was ready for a convertible ride in the mountains, as opposed to a workday on a slow Friday. He greeted me with a big smile.

"Have a seat, Lisette," he said, motioning to a nice leather chair pulled out in front of his desk. Sinking into the rich leather, I waited to hear why he summoned me to an impromptu meeting.

"I wanted to have a quick conversation with you regarding the advertising contest, and who we are choosing as the winner and why. The why is the important part, and part of the reason I wanted to have a face-to-face discussion with you." He stared at me fixedly, and I gulped. *I didn't get the PP account. He wants to make sure I know why I wasn't the one chosen, and let me down easy. Remember, keep smiling no matter what, and don't let your disappointment show. It is simply business Liz, nothing more.*

"I want you to know it was a really tough decision. All three had a strong platform to the advertising pitch, and dove into working closely with the clients in Tennessee. Making it to the top three will open doors within Burke and Bradley, no doubt about it," he continued. I was nervously toying with one of my rings, trying to stay calm and composed. I bit my lip in anticipation as I held my breath.

"That being said, you were the one I chose to head up this project with me. You're the winner, Lisette, and I wanted to pull you in here because I had a feeling you would over-think this wonderful accolade, and believe it had something to do with making up for the whole fiasco in Tennessee. I want to clear up any misconceptions with you on that aspect.

"Number one, nothing can wipe the weekend's slate clean in my mind. Nothing could make up for or excuse their behavior. Good to know they came back with glowing reviews about you. In fact, both Judson Sr. and Jr. had nothing but great things to say, so I'm not brushing a bad review under the rug in an attempt to smooth over the whole thing. I'm also not choosing you to placate the situation. I want to emphasize this: independent of their votes, I would have chosen you regardless of their feedback. Reason being—you got up on the stage and simply wowed us. It was clear to me from the beginning, because your passion was evident. You were confident, collected; you had a vision, and wove your vision into a true advertising story. You had the evidence to support your findings, and I believe I could put you in front of any client, and you could sell them.

Your masterful delivery, your poise, your presence on stage, and how you work face-to-face with a client, all played a part in getting you this well-deserved role. I needed to choose someone who could walk into a room side by side with me, and hold her own. In fact, I need someone who would bring something extra to the table, and I knew early on you're the person I had been looking for from the start." Will finished his pitch, and waited for my response. He leaned back in his chair, folding his arms, and looking intently at me.

I struggled to find the appropriate words. "Will, I can hardly think of what to say, which is rare because my role in this business is to find the right words in any situation." I took in a deep breath, letting it sink in. *He chose me, he chose me, oh my gosh, he chose me!* My thoughts could hardly contain themselves. I had to remember not to shriek with glee until I left his office.

"I can't thank you enough for choosing me, this is unexpected and wonderful. I am on cloud nine, and so humbled by this opportunity and by your kind words. I promise I will work tirelessly on this account, and will do everything in my power to make sure you never regret this decision. I am so thrilled to get started. Thank you again, this really is a career-defining moment for me. *I'm speechless.*" I managed to get out those words, and hoped they conveyed even a sliver of how I was feeling inside at the great news.

"I'm glad you're excited, I was hoping to talk about some of the details with you before I leave for a work trip. Are you free at the end of day? We could do a working happy hour, and toast your success." He grinned good-naturedly, and I could feel my insides turning to mush—basking in the glow of his charm and gladiator good looks.

"Sure, works great for me. Let me know where." I could hardly restrain the giddy schoolgirl inside me.

"I'll have Max set it up at someplace close by, and get you the details. Bring your portfolio for the account, and we can discuss, also bring names of any team members you want to work with on the project." Now he stood and came around to my chair. He held out a hand, which I gently took, and he led me to his office door where he put his hand on the small of my back.

"See you soon, Lisette, I'm expecting great things from you." When he winked at me, I could have crumbled into a million little pieces, but somehow I magically made my feet move me back to my desk. I sat down in a daze. Max was now talking with Cat and Jason, and they were headed towards Will's office to hear the news they were turned down. I wished I could see Jason's face at the news. I felt badly that Cat didn't get the opportunity though. I made a promise to myself, if they actually gave me input on the team, I would make sure to pull her in. Her raw talent would be a huge help to get the account off the ground. I gulped as I shakily tried to drink some water to calm my nerves.

My next challenge was to figure out a way to stay focused until we met for happy hour. It was going to be tough.

CHAPTER 12

After work, I walked into the dimly lit bar, and saw Will sitting on a stool by the bar.

Walking briskly toward me, he said, "I noticed some employees from Burke and Bradley near the back. I hate to change locations on you, but I think it might help us talk more freely about the account team if we went to a more private location. Would you mind?" I shot a glance towards the back of the bar, and saw a handful of familiar faces. The last thing I wanted was to have everyone talking about seeing Superman and me out together, so I immediately agreed.

"Yes, Will, but where can we go that is private? All of the bars and restaurants around here are typical favorites for the staff, and we could run into someone anywhere we go."

"I do know of one place. It is private, and has an excellent view. It is a little off the beaten path though." He eyed me warily.

"Sounds perfect, where is it?"

"Well, it's my place. I have a whole assortment of drinks, and it would just be to talk about work. It is the first place I thought of where we would be free of any unwanted Burke and Bradley colleagues' attention. Lisette, it is completely your call on this one." His hypnotic eyes were pulling me in. *Eek, his place, we are really going to Superman's place? Could a girl get so lucky? I'm so nervous I'm afraid I'm going to puke. Relax, Liz, it is only business.*

I nodded, and added what I hoped was a confident response. We quickly slipped out of the bar unnoticed, and into his car in the underground private lot.

He drove us into another underground lot where we parked his car. It was the nicest underground lot I had ever seen, with its own security staff who knew him by name. From the outside, the main entrance was a huge stone archway, with a heavy-duty security panel allowing you inside the doorway to the main security desk where two men wearing guns monitored the building's comings and goings. It was the most secure condo building I had ever encountered.

The elevator required a special key code in order to access the floor where William had his condo.

Walking into the main entrance I was enchanted by the high ceilings, and saw a case for awards and accolades from Burke and Bradley, and also Will's time as a rugby player. The entertaining room was floor-to-ceiling glass, with dark red tanned leather chairs, sofas, and lounge chairs, all with a certain vintage art deco look. It was all tastefully decorated and designed, which made me wonder if he pulled all of this together, or if he enlisted the help of a professional design team. This was straight out of a magazine highlighting lifestyles of the rich and famous. Walking around the place made me nervous because I didn't want to scuff anything, or bring in dirt to the meticulously arranged surroundings.

Oh my, I quickly learned he owned the entire floor. I couldn't fathom what a monthly payment on that piece of property would look like. Probably more than I make in a year.

During the quick tour, I noticed every piece of furniture and pieces of art followed a theme of clean lines, pristine white walls, and rich wood accents. His main room had a fireplace, with soft white sofas on a light brown rug covering the gorgeous wood floors. The bathroom had a Jacuzzi and a shower with clear glass surrounding it, with no curtain. *Hmmm... full view of anyone showering. Get your mind out of the gutter, Liz.*

Every window showed a breathtaking view of the city's skyscrapers. His condo was higher than most of the surrounding buildings, and if he didn't have the very top floor, it was pretty darn close. In the distance, I could see Lake Michigan behind all of the gorgeous buildings breaking up the view of the horizon.

His master bedroom was gorgeous. The floor-to-ceiling windows and cathedral ceiling gave me a sense of floating among the tops of the buildings and clouds. The room's curtains could close off the entire wall with the click of a button. Not like anyone would be able to see into his place from that height, but in case he felt like he wanted a little extra privacy, it was a nice option. A balcony wrapped around his condo.

The kitchen was filled with shiny black appliances, and a huge island for extra storage. It opened up into his dining area, and had extra seating around the walls. He had black-and-white antique photos representing artists, authors, poets, visionaries, and inventors adorning his walls. It was quite the collection, perfectly placed and spaced. I noticed Ernest Hemingway, Bob Dylan, Charlotte Bronte, Ralph Waldo Emerson, Dale Carnegie, F. Scott Fitzgerald, Robert Frost, Jack Kerouac, Edgar Allen Poe, J.D. Salinger, Hunter S. Thompson, Henry David Thoreau, and Walt Whitman. On a closer inspection I noticed pictures of buildings or people from some of the most influential ad agencies over the past fifty years, such as Young and Rubicam, Cramer-Krasselt, and Leo Burnett. The whole compilation was impressive.

Of course, Will had his own wine closet, which was stocked with bottles from around the world. Although it was technically a closet, it smelled like a wine cellar, with temperature controls to preserve the aging bottles.

The opulence and glamour of the whole place made me feel entirely out of my element. I wondered what a place like this would cost?

"Not quite the typical bachelor pad, is it? Your place is amazing, Will, truly exquisite." What I had seen had definitely painted a picture of elegant taste and decadence.

"Lisette, this is where I hang my hat. Would you like some wine? I have some chilling."

"Sure, thank you." I sensed he was aware I was a little ill at ease at the surroundings.

"Please make yourself at home, "Mi casa es su casa." I'll pour you a little wine to make sure you like it, and then feel free to pour yourself a glass. I'm going to grab some of the files from my office, and will be right back." I nodded as he strode off down another uninvestigated hallway; perhaps where he had a study or an amazing library of sorts. I was beginning to feel a little like a fish out of water being in such a nice place. After I poured myself a healthy glass of wine, I pulled a chair out from his gorgeous glass dining room table. Waiting for him to return, I sipped the delicate wine as I gazed around the space. Once he got back, he poured himself a glass, and then sat across from me. He started talking about work, and I asked him about some of the other new business clients he romanced into coming to Burke and Bradley. Our conversation was easy and a natural, back-and-forth playful banter. When we tired of work talk, we joked around. I found out he likes sherbet, and trying to be handy at his lake house, but he isn't very good at it, he has a secret love of the TV show "Dukes of Hazard," but didn't watch the movie, and he can't stand Brussels sprouts because he once ate one raw as a kid, and couldn't get past the experience in later years.

Then Will motioned for me to share, and I shared all kinds of personal things. I told him how I can't believe sherbet was an actual ice cream flavor because I couldn't fathom someone deciding it belongs in the ice cream family. I once bought all the materials needed to learn how to knit, and then lost interest. I secretly like old mystery shows like "Twin Peaks" and "The X-Files," and I can't stand raisin cookies.

We laughed for what seemed like hours, talking about random topics as the wine flowed. When Will opened another bottle of wine, he asked if I wanted to taste it before pouring a whole glass; then he left the kitchen to find some snacks for us in the pantry room.

Walking over to the kitchen island, I realized I was shaking with nerves. It happens to me every time I secretly first like someone, and I can't stop myself from trembling slightly. I poured myself another dab of wine, and due to my annoying shakes, I spilled some on his gorgeous granite countertop. Feeling immediately guilty about the mishap, I started looking around for a towel I could use to clean it up. I didn't see anything readily available, so in my embarrassment, when he reappeared, I had to ask, "William, I am so sorry. I spilled a bit of wine on your counter. Do you have something I can use to take care of it?" My cheeks were flushing crimson again. With Superman looking so masculine and muscular with his jacket off, and his open white-collared shirt offsetting his tanned muscular neck and biceps, I could hardly think straight. He came up to me as I stood by the sink. I could smell him, a mixture of his familiar cologne and pine blend, always masculine and woodsy. It was almost overwhelming.

"Lisette, jeez, you're shaking." As he put his hands on my shoulders to steady me, he asked, "Are you okay? You're trembling. Are you cold? Let me get you my jacket." My body was trembling without control, and I couldn't make myself relax. It was a heady mixture of nerves at being inside this gorgeous man's place, on top of being wildly turned on by him, which only seemed intensified by the wine consumption. I was also amazed at how easy our conversation had been all night. Every time I had a chance to spend time with this man, I was more intrigued and delighted by what I found. The mind-altering combination sent my senses into overdrive. As he started to go to find me a jacket, I instinctively grabbed his shirt close to his waist to stop him from turning away. He turned towards me, halted by my action, as his spellbinding eyes pierced mine, waiting for me to speak. *Liz, you're grabbing his clothes, what are you thinking! Abort, let go of the poor man!*

Immediately realizing what I was doing, I quickly released my hand. "No, I'm fine really—the excitement of tonight and everything, and being here, my mind is simply in overdrive. I honestly don't know why I am shaking. I'm fine though, I don't need anything really..." I trailed off, lost in what to say, sucked into the depth of his disarming gaze. I think I would have stopped breathing if my body didn't continue doing it for me. Looking at his perfectly chiseled features took me away from my body and senses.

He was closely studying my face, debating if I was telling him the whole truth. My body was still visibly trembling, rebuking my attempts to get myself under control. The mixture of being in his place, the smell of him surrounding me, in conjunction with the wine, put devious thoughts in my head—thoughts I should fight, but which nonetheless make me incredibly nervous, and somehow more self-conscious about being in these intimate surroundings with him.

Will rubbed my arms lightly, still studying my face. He retrieved a comfy sweatshirt from the chair where he had tossed it, and draped it around my shoulders.

"In case you're still cold," he murmured, his voice making a deep, throaty and heavenly sound. "Plus I will feel better if you have this on. I can't tell whether you're just being polite. As my guest you're welcome to anything at my place, including a jacket." He grinned, and his smile had such a disarming effect on me, it was hard to keep my thoughts straight, and maintain my professional persona. When I tried picking up my wine, I realized my hand would be too unsteady, so I put it back down, and played with my thumb ring instead. Will was uncomfortably close, and still watching me, so I forced a smile.

"Are you sure you're okay, you're still shaking." William whispered, moving closer to me. Now he was standing directly in front of me, close enough to reach out and touch. He was looking at me, a look I have never seen before. His steely eyes and rugged features easily hiding his true emotions, but being so close was like being close to a volcano, I could feel the energy erupting from him. He slowly leaned down, and with one hand, he cupped my chin as he bent down, and his face moved closer. I was frozen in place, hardly daring to move as his lips moved closer to mine. Time was at a standstill as I realized Will was about to kiss me.

His kiss was incredibly gentle, like a soft caress. My lips tingled the moment they connected with his, and it was like I was instantly cloaked in a blanket of warmth. I could feel my resolve softening under his kiss, so I stood up onto my tiptoes in order to snuggle closer against him. His arms were pulling me in, and completely encompassing me in a full embrace. I could feel my body reacting to him as I let myself get swallowed up in his presence, tingling spreading from between my legs to my entire being. My body's response to him was unlike anything I had ever experienced before. I could feel a heart-stopping sensation move from my lips to the tips of my fingers to the end of my toes, and all the way back to the top of my head.

His soft kisses turned more fierce and passionate as we both yearned for more. We clutched each other as our lips connected, his hands moving all over my body, lingering on the small of my back to cupping my butt, and gently caressing down the side of my legs, and back. The warmth from his hands felt like magic to my cool skin. We moved out of the kitchen into the main living room area. The heat between us began to grow as his mere touch created pure electricity within me. I groaned as his kisses moved over my neck and chest. All I could think was how desperately I wanted him, ever since the moment of our first chance meeting, to when I ran into him again at my new job. My body was telling me that I had always desperately needed him—and needed this very moment. Everything about him was perfect, and to me he embodied what I think a man should be—the ideal of masculinity in the flesh.

Our passion carried us over to the couch, his jacket sliding off my slender shoulders as pure animal instinct took over. I grabbed the buttons of his shirt as I straddled him, fumbling with his shirt buttons as I fiercely kissed him, every moment feeling right, our hands and lips begging for more. Pulling his white shirt off him revealed his tanned abs, and I realized with glee my suspicions were correct. After all of the times I marveled at what his body might look like under his shirts, I finally knew with certainty he was absurdly ripped. I couldn't help but bite my lip as I etched my fingers over the ridges of his defined stomach and chest. He felt smooth and warm to my touch as I moved my hands eagerly over his entire body. He grabbed the bottom of my shirt and pulled it over my head, flinging it to the floor.

Will, now shirtless, said raggedly as he gazed at me in wonder, as I straddled him on the couch, "You know how I said I didn't know if we should do this type of thing?"

"Yeah?" I panted.

"Let's agree to agree I was wrong. I want you, Lisette. I can't hide anymore from the fact I can't stop thinking about you." Then he flipped me around so he was on top, and I sunk deliciously into the soft cushions as he started unbuckling his belt. He paused, hungrily taking me in with his eyes.

"Are you sure this is okay? Is this what you want, Lisette? I don't want to do anything you're not comfortable with, and I will respect whatever you choose. I don't want us rushing into anything." He looked so solemn, his stunning eyes searching mine, his gorgeous golden body etched to perfection with taut muscles. His chest heaving, I thought I might drool as I watched his formed chest and abs move up and down. His look of concern was so touching, and it was strangely reassuring that he would stop to make sure I was okay. It didn't take me long to think it over, being this near to him made any reservations fade away. I felt safe with him, and everything felt right.

"Yes, I want this," I replied softly, realizing the moment I said it, it was the truth. Typically I was the girl who wanted to wait, who needed to wait, but with the crazy bizarre situations we were in together, I felt like we had built a bond so strong, that I felt completely comfortable with the idea of being with him. *I honestly can't devour him with my eyes any longer, and not have him, not with what we have been through together, I don't think I could stand it.*

He stepped closer, and wrapped his arms around my waist

so our legs were touching, and his groin was pressed up against me. I could feel his desire.

"I want you to convince me," he said as his expression now turned into one of mischief. His lips curled into a good-natured grin. He leaned over me, his hard chest and muscles were inches away from my own. I could feel my heart racing, his masculine scent filling my head. "Convince me," he whispered, as he playfully nibbled my lower lip. Then he kissed my collarbone and down to my breasts. "I'm waiting," he murmured between kisses. It was getting hard to concentrate, and my breath was coming quicker.

"Hmmm," I murmured, "Do you always get what you want?" His devious grin made me think he did. After I took a deep breath, I whispered, "I want this," repeating it, this time louder, "I want this, and I want you. I know I want you because every time I see you, I have to remember to breathe." I paused, feeling unsure in this new uncertain territory. He rewarded me with gentle kisses moving down my body.

"Will, you make me nervous, in a good way, but I do feel safe around you. You were very protective when we went to Tennessee, and I have never before experienced someone caring about me so much, and it was a nice feeling. I know you're a good guy. Anyone who would leave their party to drop off a purse, and then kick out the hoodlum who is giving two girls grief, all out of the kindness of his heart, can't be all bad. In fact, I'm willing to bet you're one of the good ones. Plus, you have a body Superman would envy." Using my own private nickname for him, I hoped he would find my response satisfactory. He was still straddling me on the couch, but his expression was hard to read because he was looking somewhat solemn again, and a little sad.

Will moved close enough so that I could literally extend a finger and touch him, and as he peered down at me, I could see the muscles around his jaw were clenched. "I can't help but be protective of you, Lisette, you're this beautiful woman who keeps getting hurt by people, and I'm really sorry you had to deal with any of it. You don't have to worry about anything happening to you when you're with me, okay?" He was searching my eyes. "It is the truth, Lisette. You are so incredibly beautiful and special. Someone should have been caring for you and protecting you, and telling you this every day. You deserve to feel safe, and cared for, I'm sorry you never had that before. I have never met anyone like you, you're truly one of a kind, and it saddens me because you have had to wait so long to hear someone say that to you." He looked honestly sad as he peered into my eyes.

His words were so sincere, which surprised me. I thought we were playing a coy game with one another. The surge of emotion I felt when he spoke so gently and softly surprised me, and I tried to push the feeling back down. My eyes started to tear up, and as I tried my best to vanquish them, one lone tear rolled down the side of my cheek. Not saying anything, he gently wiped my tear away with such tenderness it only made me want him more as he leaned in and kissed me deeply. He pulled me gently off the couch and onto his expansive balcony. Several chairs and couches, plus a table, were set up out there, all high enough where no one could see us, and kept us hidden from view. The evening was slightly mild with an occasional light, cool breeze. He kissed me deeply as we stood on his dark balcony with the soft glow of light hitting us from inside his suite. He undid the button of my jeans, and I slid them off.

I could see the stars shining in the late night sky, and I felt like we were on a floating platform since I couldn't see anything below unless I walked up to the edge. He threw a large blanket from one of the couches on the floor so we had a spot. He was being so gentle and sweet. He slowly took off all of my clothes, and gazed down at me. Behind his half-naked body, I could see thousands of stars in the night sky. Their light blended warmly with the low glow of the city lights off in the distance. With Will kneeling above me on the blanket, with the breathtaking backdrop, I felt like I was in a scene from a movie. His looked at me admiringly, his eyes slowly traveling up and down my figure. And I couldn't help but wonder what he was thinking.

"Lisette, you are really stunning. You are beautiful, and I want to kiss every inch of you, if you'll let me." His wicked grin made all of my reservations, or doubts about what he would think of me nude, faded away into nothingness. I couldn't help but grin as I reached up and kissed him, starting on his chest, working down to his defined "V" muscles at the bottom of his abs. He groaned, and started to slowly tease me with his fingers.

"Hmmm, you're already warm, Lisette. But I'm not going to rush this; all good things come to those who wait." I could feel my pulse quickening as he worked magic with his fingers, making me crazy with desire, which was becoming more intense by the second. I needed him, but he was taking his time.

He wrapped my legs around him, and lifted me to one of the comfy chairs on the patio, and pulled me forward to the edge. He moved his masterful hands along my skin, stopping at my breasts and then continuing down, delicately licking and sucking. I tilted my head back in pure ecstasy, becoming fully frantic with need. His sensual mouth had me on the brink. I clasped my hands on either side of the chair, but Will stood up and moved my hands so they were over my head, clasping the back of the chair. He moved my body again so I was right on the edge.

"Keep your hands there, Lisette, trust me," he instructed, teasing me with light kisses. Now I was writhing with need, and twisting anxiously in the chair. My position allowed my hips to move more freely, and kept my release at bay as I was fully extending and clutching the chair.

"William, oh Will, I'm so close," I breathed, and he stopped and stood up. Looking at me like a lion in the wild, he smiled and slowly turned me around in the chair and came behind me. I could smell his cologne as he moved, and in his eyes I could see his desire for me. His other hand pulled my hair to the side as he zealously started kissing and lightly nibbling my neck. I groaned out loud, it was too much. My whole body was a slave to the feeling, to this thirst that needed quenching.

His movements became quicker, and I could feel the delicious warmth from his palm and his fingers as he explored my body. I could feel his hands creating a pulsating urge inside me, followed by a feeling of pure elation. I arched my back, and let the release take me. I moaned as it consumed me, basking in the afterglow of the sensation.

Will turned me around to face him. "Was that good for you?" He raised an eyebrow with the question. He gazed down, peering at me from behind his lashes and sexy, disheveled hair. He was grinning, and I couldn't help but give him a taste of his own medicine.

"Oh yeah," I purred, "but what about you? I hear you like to have to wait," I teased, and kneeled down on the blanket as I started to return the favor. He was perfect, standing in front of me as I wrapped my hands around him. I moved my mouth across his body, changing the tempo and technique occasionally, I was taking cues from him on what he liked, and how to please him. He leaned his head back and moaned. *He is liking everything so far.*

It was quite the picture, a man with dark features and movie-quality looks standing naked on the balcony with nothing behind him other than the dazzling stars brightening the night sky like lights on a Christmas tree. A light breeze graced us by cooling the midnight air. As he grew more excited, I stood and soundlessly moved him to the chair.

I sat him down, and then coyly said, "Make sure to leave your hands on the top of this chair. Trust me, Will." A grin crept across my face, and I went down on him again as he looked at me with astonishment and amusement, but he kept his hands where I had directed. After I felt like he was close to the breaking point. I slowly stood and straddled him again.

Will stopped me. "I want to make sure we are being safe, Lisette," he murmured. Being a "double-protection" girl, I smiled back.

"Couldn't agree more, I'm on the pill, but Jodi likes to shove condoms in my purse when I'm not looking because she thinks it is funny. Honestly I swear I'm not the girl who carries condoms everywhere I go. My roommate is simply a little odd." He cocked his head as he grinned.

"I know you are not that type of girl, Lisette, but you're okay with this?" Looking down at him, the concern on his face gave him a boyish look, and I was more certain than ever. I nodded and kissed him lightly on the lips, and rolled the condom on with his assistance. We started moving together slowly at first, with me riding him. Refreshing gusts blew my hair away from my neck every few minutes. I pulled Will's hands away from the chair so he knew he could move them, and he grabbed my buttocks as he thrust into me, moving slowly and steady until we worked up to a feverish pace. My body was responding, and getting ready for another round. Watching the exquisite muscles in his face and body respond, he was moving his hips in a circle, getting me worked up again. I could feel him filling me completely; bringing in more warmth and desire. We moved in tandem, fully entwined and contented. I could see his beautiful face as he felt release, and slumped into him, suddenly exhausted. He pulled a blanket around me, kissing my forehead. We gazed in silence at the stars for a while.

Finally Will spoke, "You're pretty amazing, a force to be reckoned with, Lisette, and I knew it the moment I met you." He sighed with pleasant exhaustion.

I smiled inwardly, taking in the moment. I was curled up next to him, my back fitting perfectly near his chest under his arm. My head rested comfortably by the base of his neck. "Yeah, you are pretty phenomenal. I think I could gaze at these stars all night. You must love this view."

"You would be surprised; I don't come out here unless I have guests. I have not had guests in a long time," he said, gazing skyward.

"I find that surprising, Will, I bet every girl you bring out here loves this. Who wouldn't? With a place like this, I think I would be entertaining all the time." Once the words were out of my mouth, I realized it could sound like I was prying.

"I *don't* bring girls out here. Whatever you thought of me before, Lisette, is probably wrong. I'm not quite the playboy you expected me to be. After a while I got bored chasing meaningless sex." Suddenly he looked down at me, pulling me in closer. "You're anything but boring, in case you were going to ask." He flashed me another grin, and I felt warmth inside again. I wasn't really sure what to do next, realizing I was still naked, cuddling with him under the blanket. I moved to get up and grab my clothes. I could feel him watching me as I pulled on my shirt, and found my bra strewn by the edge of the balcony.

"Good thing this wasn't an inch closer to the edge, or someone would have had a surprise to find a bra outside their door when leaving tomorrow morning."

"You should stay the night, Lisette, really. We can watch a movie, and relax." He was studying my face as I stood very still, contemplating the request. "You don't have to question what just happened; we don't have to talk about what it means, and what it doesn't mean. Let's be together tonight, and let things get complicated another day. What do you say? Plus, then you don't have to drive home, it's late and who knows who is on the road at this hour. You should stay, Lisette, unless of course you really don't want to." The last part was punctuated with his signature grin, while his smoldering eyes took in my reaction to his plea.

I dared not hope anything would come of this, nor let my

mind wander to what it could mean, and what it didn't mean. I didn't want to think about it either, and couldn't let myself think of this as anything more than it was. No wandering down the endless path of questioning and doubts, hopes and theories—because I couldn't risk my heart.

His reaction made perfect sense. He was asking for a night, a night where we could be together, and not worry about anything else. Tonight we would not worry about our situation getting awkward, creating chaos at work, or the possibility of others finding out—or the fact this could turn into nothing, and the repercussions of the nothingness—or this turning into something, and the aftermath of this being something. We would not deal with the possibility that this carried more meaning than we realize, or this could ruin our business relationship. As important, it was about me worrying I'd compare every guy I'd ever meet to William Duke, never meeting anyone who compares to him in my whole life, him going on a date with a model tomorrow, and all the other exhausting possibilities our minds could spew at us would have to wait for another time. Pushing those devilish thoughts out of my mind, I took what he said to heart. We don't have to think about what it means or doesn't mean, because we don't have to dig into it now. We can let it get complicated another day. He asked me to stay so the two of us can be together tonight, so I stayed.

In the morning, I woke up in a bundle of deliciously soft silk sheets that smelled like Will. At first my eyes, still groggy, wondered where I was, but the smell brought me back. His scent brought back flashes of the ecstasy from last night, and I felt warm and tingly inside all over again. I reached over to the other side of the bed to Will, but I realized I was alone in his spacious room. I quickly got up and put on my clothes, wondering if he had left in the night. *Oh no, does he regret this? Did he try to leave me, and realized this was his place, and pretended he needed to dash? Did I overstay my welcome? What if things are forever weird between us?* These thoughts and more rambled through my head as I grabbed my bag from the floor, and dashed out the room, expecting to run through the front door and slink out a side entrance in embarrassment. When I saw the kitchen, I skidded to a halt.

Will was standing over the stove shirtless with the best-looking guy sweats I had ever seen *in my life.* My mouth opened slightly as he turned around, and I saw the distinct V muscles by his waist, and his etched-to-perfection biceps and abs, with his hair looking deliciously disheveled. He had a frying pan in one hand, and pancake batter in another.

"Would you like a quick bite before you start your day, Lisette? I make a mean pancake. Come on, put your stuff down and stay a while." He disarmed me with his smile, and once again, I had let my thoughts run amuck. The thought gleefully dawned on me—the guy who was so scrumptious he could melt butter on toast had asked me to stay twice within twelve hours, and for a second time, I couldn't help but say yes.

CHAPTER 13

Jodi was waiting for me when I got back to the apartment after enjoying Will's scrumptious breakfast.

"So, someone ended up staying the night." She said to me with a mischievous smile. "Details. Spill!" She was sitting pretzel legged in our couch, holding a cup of coffee.

"Yes, I stayed the night. You know I typically need definitions and conversations about what everything means before I take it to the next step with a guy, but things are different with him. This whole situation is a new one for me. Ultimately, he appealed to the carefree side of me, and convinced me to spend the whole night with him. I'm not over-thinking it though, Jodi, I don't have any preconceived notions about us. In fact I'm convinced nothing can come of this, because this is *the* William Duke we are talking about. It was something fun for one night, and maybe that's the end of it!" I started cleaning up in the kitchen area as Jodi studied me.

"Liz, it's great you're finally letting yourself have some fun—to be more like me in that respect," Jodi said, with a gloating smile.

"I don't know if I would go that far. You're not forgetting the nasty cut I got from Ben, one of your infamous nights of living carefree, are you?"

"Oh Liz, you know I apologized a million times over. Plus, we got a gorgeous picture frame out of the whole ordeal. Speaking of that though, I could have sworn I saw Ben driving past our house the other day. It was the weirdest thing. I was coming in with some groceries, and a big beat-up red truck drove by, and as I turned around to look back, I immediately thought I saw him looking back at me from the driver's seat. I kid you not, but it probably was some guy who looked like him." She went back to nonchalantly flipping through her magazine.

"You're serious, you thought it looked like him? Pretty wild thought, but you're right, a lot of people who look like him could be passing by." I could feel goose bumps forming on my arms at the thought it of being him, and the ugliness of what had happened. I shivered at what could have happened if Will had not shown up when he did.

"So, Liz, what is next for your big project? Are you going anywhere fun, when do you start shooting and getting the images shot for the advertising campaigns?"

"We did talk about the project this morning when he made me breakfast." I said nonchalantly as I washed a dish.

"Get out of town, he made you breakfast? He didn't kick you out super early for the walk of shame, instead he cooked for you?"

"Yeah, but I don't think it was a big deal or anything. He was already making breakfast for himself, and he didn't have to rush into work since it was a Saturday morning. It wasn't really a huge deal, however, it was fantastic. He made eggs, bacon, and pancakes with strawberries on top. It was really out of this world." I couldn't help but smile at the thought of it. *Not to mention the sight of him shirtless in those butt-hugging sweats, me coming up behind him in the morning sliding my fingers down those etched abs. The eggs were not the only scrumptious thing on the menu—and we had seconds of both this morning—but a girl can keep some details a secret.*

"It was out of this world, huh, and are you talking about the sex or the pancakes?" Jodi shot me one of her infectious smiles, making me blush. "I'm just giving you a hard time, and honestly the whole night sounds amazing. Do you think someone like him has those breakfast goodies on hand, or do you think he got it in preparation of seeing you?" Jodi arched an eyebrow at her own question, wondering if this was a preplanned overnight rendezvous.

I couldn't help but shake an unsettling feeling. "Jodi, you're making it sound like a scene from a movie where he deliberately planned for me to stay over. You're letting your imagination run away with you." But deep down, even as I said it, I started to doubt my own convictions. *What if he did know I would come home with him, and it was all planned? What if I was the foregone conclusion, another conquest or notch in his belt? Did I become the girl I promised myself I would never become? He was trying to convince me he is not the playboy type everyone makes him out to be, but at this point I can't be certain.*

The whole notion made me slightly sick to my stomach, so I forced my thoughts elsewhere.

"Back to your earlier question, we will be going to Florida next to start shooting before we move the shoot to an international location. They are still fleshing out the details, and I am one small part of this whole creative team Will is pulling together for the pitch. This could be a huge account for us, and since I'm so new to the team I really feel I'm going along to learn more than anything else. I should know once we are in Florida what the next steps will be. They want to do some of the basic ad stuff in Florida, and then the commercials and extended campaign abroad. I am one of many going, so who knows if I will have much time to see him?" I said honestly, but I secretly hoped we would be able to find some time together. I couldn't get him out of my mind, and the night on the balcony was surreal.

"What about him? Liz, you're skimping on all the gory details. Did he rock your world, and was he everything you would have imagined?" She bit her lip expectantly, I'm sure she was thinking of every romance novel she ever read. I'm not a kiss-and-tell type of person, but this was Jodi who was like a sister to me, so I had to tell her something. Plus knowing we had the night we did, and not being able to say anything to anyone, had me busting at the seams.

"The sexual chemistry was out of this world, Jodi." I had this huge grin as Jodi poured us some mimosas so she could get me to continue gushing.

"Tell me *everything*..." I took a deep breath, and got ready for what would undoubtedly be an afternoon of several mimosas, and a lot of girl talk.

CHAPTER 14

Back at the office on Monday the word had spread that my pitch was the one selected. A lot of people stopped by and congratulated me, which was all a little overwhelming. I went from this relative unknown to the main water-cooler topic of conversation. Becoming the hot topic at the office definitely took me out of my comfort zone in a big way.

What a surprise. A dozen red roses were delivered to the office mid-morning. My heart was in my throat. Could they be from Will? Yikes, the card said they were from Phil Burns. Phil, a notorious womanizer, reminded me of every TV character who had a quick smile and constant drink in their hand. Salt-and-pepper, well-groomed hair, always slightly tanned and in shape, his grin could melt ice, and frequently won deals if women were involved in the decision. With the men, it wouldn't surprise me if he wined and dined them, and then took them to a shooting range or strip joint. Such stories floated around the office, and he was definitely old school in his approach to winning business.

Phil wrote on the card, "Way to win it, kid, congrats on the first step in what I am sure will be a successful career." – Phil. Yes, the gesture was incredibly nice, but I couldn't help but feel slightly disappointed.

Max walked by wearing trendy suit pants with suspenders, his white shirt sleeves rolled up, with a little stubble on his face. Seeing the roses, he stopped, "Liz, who is the mystery sender of those beautiful roses?"

"Um, it was Phil, congratulating me on winning the competition." I said bashfully, not used to getting flowers, much less being the center of attention.

"Ah, lucky girl," Max said with an eyebrow raised, as he sauntered off to his desk.

Jason walked over, his black hair greased back so thick you could see your reflection in the mounds of product he slathered on his head that morning. He approached me with an oily grin, then paused at my desk with his arms folded, and his face contorted with anger.

"Who *are* the flowers from Liz? Perhaps you ended up making more of an *impression* on the Judson boys than you're admitting to the rest of us, eh?" Putting both hands on my desk, he leaned in closer.

I ignored the comment and his lecherous stare, as he continued, "What did you do to win the account, Liz? Did you meet up with Judson Jr. afterwards, and give him a little something to remember you by? Are those flowers from him? I deserved that account Liz. I worked my butt off for that account, and here you are barely a full day in your new desk, and yet you're winning the top account spot. It doesn't add up, Liz, I don't see it, and I don't appreciate it. I think some shady shit is going on, and I'm going to find out what it is. Did you blow him? Did you? Do you expect your looks, and those lips to get you where you need to go? I saw your pitch, so I know you didn't win on your own merits. Perhaps you decided to use some of the other talents God gave you to win this thing?" Beads of sweat were forming by his brow, the stench of stale coffee and cigarettes wafted from his mouth as he practically spat out the words.

Leaning as far back in the chair as I could, his nearness made me feel purely nauseous. The nerve of this guy, of all the low-down demeaning things to say, he chose the worst. I paused, letting my mind race through all of the horrible things I could say back, but I made sure to mentally cross out some of them. I wanted to be deliberate and impactful with what I said next.

"If you remember, Jason, I asked you to make sure Judson Jr. was nowhere near me, and you threw him directly in my path. Frankly, I don't care what you do with your butt, but as far I'm concerned, someone as conniving and disgusting as you does not deserve an opportunity like this. I don't appreciate the implication, I don't like you leaning on my desk, and your breath smells like something that crawled out of a rotting sewer." His eyes widened in shock at the words that were coming out of my mouth like daggers. I stood up so I was looking down at him as he leaned on my desk.

"Here is what I am going to do, Jason. I am going to do you a favor; I'm going to pretend we never had this little chat. But if you ever so much as walk in the vicinity of my desk again, I'm going to go to HR and see what they have to say about your little theories and comments. Would Burke and Bradley want to risk keeping someone like you on the payroll, since you obviously get your jollies from harassing and intimidating your female counterparts? They will not appreciate your sexual innuendos, your comments regarding my work, and what you suggested I did to one of the Judsons. What do you think they would have to say? Choose you words carefully now, Jason." I smiled politely at him. My fists were tightly balled up and hidden from view, and I had to control my mood. No way did I want him to have any sense that he had ruffled my feathers. I wanted *the upper hand.*

Jason slowly removed his hands from my desk, and stood up. Grinding his teeth with frustration, and I could see the wheels turning in his puny head as he debated replying with something hideous. I was pleased because instead, he turned on his heels and stormed away. *Win one for Lizzie.* I thought to myself, as I tried to control my shaking. Today I had officially made an enemy in the office, when I barely knew enough people to call my friends.

The next day a note from Will arrived, saying in two days he would be back in the office, and wanted to go through a final review of who else I wanted to include in my creative team going to Florida. He threw out a few possibilities, Jason being one of them, and said he looked forward to discussing it with me. His email was formal and direct, but a few other people on the account team were included on the email as well for their visibility so he had to be completely professional and aloof. I was started to feel a yearning to see him again—alone. Our brief encounter was starting to feel more and more like it was some wonderful dream, and I needed to feel close to him again to remind myself it had truly happened.

My thoughts were interrupted as Cat stopped by my desk. She pulled her thick gypsy-like hair in a big ponytail at the top of her head as she squinted at me, and put her hands on her hips. "Is Jason bothering you? He is such a creep. I hope you're not taking anything he says to heart. I thought your presentation was outstanding, and you deserved it. Don't let him bring you down."

I couldn't help but smile in response to her kindness. "Thanks Cat, I really appreciate it. I honestly think you deserved the spot, you're incredibly talented, which I hope you know. As for Jason, I don't know why he can't stand me. Yes I'm new, and he didn't win this time, but I'm sure he has won plenty of times before, and he is obviously making a name for himself. Yes, he's a complete creep, but I still don't like the feeling that I've made an enemy in the office." I cringed at our recent battle of wits and words.

"Yeah, Jason has always been a poor sport, but I have never seen him like this. Rumor is he stayed up night after night working on his pitch and presentation. Normally his ego makes it difficult for his head to fit through doors, but I think adding to the mix the fact he was really trying this time, pushed him over the edge. He'll get over it though; men can be such babies sometimes. Let me know if you ever need to blow off some steam. With a great place around the corner, and I am game for a good happy hour." She gave me a good-natured smile, and after I thanked her again, she returned to her seat. The smell of roses wafted through the air as I started typing at my desk.

It was crazy how one moment at this job I felt like a million bucks, and the next second I felt like something you might find on the bottom of your shoe. Maybe I have to chalk it up to office politics, and keep my head down for two days until Will returned—the one thing I was really looking forward to. I have to be inconspicuous until then—and it won't be easy.

Two days later Max walked over with a little envelope he dropped gingerly onto my desk. "Special delivery for you, Lisette," he said with a wink as he scurried on with his day. I couldn't help but feel the colors rise in my cheeks. *This must be from William.*

Inside the envelope was a colorful Florida card, which made me wonder where Max had to go to find a card with the actual state of Florida on it. The message read:

I have a late flight in tonight. Can you meet me at Aqua-Vive Vineyard at 7 p.m., in the Gold Room? Let Max know if you have a conflict. – Will.

Shivers rushed up my spine; the day couldn't fly by fast enough. *A conflict, hmmm, yes I am having a personal conflict with how giddy I get at the slight mention of his name. I'm stuck on this guy like white on rice, and I have to make sure I don't leave myself with a mess to clean up—such as my heart in a thousand tiny pieces on the floor.*

Was Will's ability to have this much impact on my mood a negative thing? I was determined to keep things very professional, and I knew that things can become dangerous when emotions get involved.

I texted Jodi to let her know I would be home late, especially because the vineyard was quite a distance from our apartment, and resolved to keep my focus the rest of the day on my final selections for those I wanted on my creative team. This meeting was, after all, about business. *That means stop drooling over Superman, Liz, and get your head in the game.*

CHAPTER 15

I marveled at the beautiful stone structure, which looked more like a building you would find in Rome than a vineyard in the Midwest. As I climbed the stairs, dwarfed by the walls, I looked down at my note with the address to make sure I was at the correct location. Walking in, everything was marble and stone, and smelled of rich wood and foliage. Plants and small trees decorated every corner, and vines were around the main reception desk. I approached the woman behind the desk, and asked where the Gold Room was located.

"Ah yes, the Gold Room is one of our finest tasting rooms. Are you Lisette?"

"Um, yes I am." *Leave it to Will to make sure the receptionist greets me in style.* He had such a way of making things seem grand and exquisite with the little things he made sure to do, or had Max do—I wasn't sure which.

The receptionist took me through a few hallways and a domed doorway. Upon entering, I knew immediately why they called it the Gold Room. The domed ceiling was painted in the style of the Sistine chapel, or the ceiling of an ancient cathedral. Gold angels and golden-robed women in Roman garb were holding crests, and standing near pillars. The room was beautifully and ornately designed, and literally transported you to Italy with its European design and lavish colors.

The back room had another domed doorway, which led outside to a covered gazebo. From this enclosed space, I had an amazing view of the vineyard off in the distance. As I scanned the room, I saw Will looking out at the scenery, casually leaning against one of the pillars, looking relaxed and at ease. I took a deep breath, and tried to calm my nerves. I cleared my throat gently so as not to startle him. He turned around and greeted me with a wide, welcoming smile, his eyes glistening.

"Hey you, it is great to see you." He gave me a big bear hug, wrapping me up in his strong arms, and making me feel like we fit perfectly together. He studied my face as he handed me a bouquet of delicate white and blue flowers, and pointed out the blue flowers.

"They are called 'Myosotis alpestris,' which is Latin for 'Forget-Me-Not.' Since it has been a while since I have seen you, I thought it was fitting. Especially when I know Phil is sending you flowers at the office, I didn't want you to forget about me." He winked, and smiled his golden heart-breaking smile, which caused me to melt.

"Will, these are lovely. I'm speechless. Even if I tried, I think it would be highly improbable to forget you—and our night. Do you have a private eye in the office? Does Max fill you in on little insignificant details about who gets flowers, and from whom, or am I special?" I couldn't help but smile back at him like a fool. My face was flushed, and I was undeniably giddy.

"Max tells me all the important things, and you getting flowers from Phil would fall under the important category. Phil can be a little... well, he's someone to be careful around, especially you." Will was suddenly looking serious, gazing sternly at me. Was he jealous? I couldn't determine what was behind his now stormy eyes.

"Will, is this jealousy I detect? I have heard stories about Phil, and I don't intend on putting myself into any situation I can't handle. I think he was honestly trying to be nice and congratulate me." I waited for Will's reaction.

Will shoved his hands in his pockets and gazed out at the vineyard again, like his thoughts were taking him far away. Something about his features hardened a little, lost in thought, and he seemed tense.

"I know joining a new company and getting noticed by executives would typically be a positive thing. Unfortunately, with Phil, sometimes other motives are at play. I should not comment on it, but I would hate for you to receive an invite from him that sounds like networking, and then have it turn into something else entirely. This might sound horribly hypocritical, and I know you don't have to believe me on this, but I don't make a habit of fraternizing with employees—I just don't.

"With you, however, I couldn't stop myself, and I debate my choice every day, and every time I question what we are doing, my will power dwindles, and I decide I need to see you. I don't know what it is about you, Lisette. Your exotic beauty and presence, are this heady mixture that can't help but attract attention. I don't ever do this type of thing, but Phil is notorious for getting friendly with female employees. And when he does, the women don't stick around long. He gets rid of them, because he can."

Will folded his arms, making his chest and arms seem larger than usual, and I felt dwarfed standing in front of him. *In the glorious shadow of my guardian angel, I could peel those clothes off him with my teeth right now.*

Will looked concerned. "I deal with him when I absolutely have to, but he is a great salesperson, and when he puts his mind to it, he represents this agency very well. He is a chameleon, and can turn into anything for anyone, and it gets us a lot of business. I can't deny it. He is in charge of wining and dining prospective clients, and unfortunately some of those tendencies bleed into other areas of the company. For reasons I can't explain, I feel very protective of you, Lisette, and it makes my skin crawl to think he could have his sights set on you. That's all." He looked at me, uncertain of whether or not the words he chose were the most well suited to explain the situation.

Will was being open and candid; he peered up from under his thick eyelashes, doubtful of the response he would receive in return. It seemed to be unfamiliar territory for him, and I could tell he was slightly ill at ease with the temperament of the conversation. I was at a loss for words. I looked down at the gorgeous flowers in my hand, and over to Will's serious face, and he seemed genuinely worried about me.

"I really appreciate your being honest with me about Phil, and I promise I will be careful around him. I think I am still reeling from the fact we are doing this, that I somehow caught your attention against all the odds. I feel like every time I'm with you, it is like I am peeling back more layers. I have to say, I'm enjoying every minute of it though, a little too much." I smiled up at him, and he took my hand in his and gently kissed it. He reached out and tilted my face towards his, and gazed at me, his hand lingering on my face. It looked like he was deep in thought, and I wished I had a way to read his mind.

"Would you like to go on a walk through the vineyard before we settle down to business? This is one of my favorite spots; they promised me we would have the place to ourselves. I can show you around if you like?" As I nodded, he placed my flowers on the table, and took my hand. He led me through a heavy arched doorway, and the metal gate clicked shut behind us. Since we were in a slightly enclosed part of the vineyard, I had not seen the immense landscape including the actual vineyard grounds, and I gasped at the view.

The vineyard was on a hill, so walking out the ornate door revealed acres of gently sloping hills with grapes planted in delicate rows. Beyond the acres of fresh, crisp green was a lake, with more rolling hills in the distance. The sun was hovering above the horizon line, casting brilliant purples and oranges onto the lake's surface, and kissed the tops of the hills in the distance. What a marvelous sight, I wondered briefly how much it had cost to reserve the best room at the vineyard, and ensure the grounds would be vacant for us.

William led me by the hand through the sloping rows. The grass in between each of the rows of grapes was soft and well manicured. When we had paused in an area where the grapes were tall enough to surely hide us from view from the main building, Will paused and pulled me towards him.

His eyes were reflecting the fading sunlight, a dance of colorful specs near his irises, and I was sucked into his gaze.

"Promise me if Phil or anyone else at the office tries anything with you, you will tell me. After the situation with the Judsons, I would feel more comfortable if I know you will be honest with me if anyone is bothering you. Agree?" He looked so pained at the thought I had to take a deep breath.

"I'm not used to someone wanting to look out for me. This is a new feeling because I'm used to relying on myself..." I started to respond as he pulled me into his warm, hard body, his arms wrapping around me, playing with my hair gently as he lightly kissed my lips. His light touch made me momentarily out of breath, yet I felt safe being this near to him, wrapped in his strong arms.

"I promise, I will," I whispered, taken in with his scent. A wonderful blending of sweet mahogany and spices mixed into his cologne, with the scent of *pure him*. He started kissing my neck. When he slowly removed my sweater, all I could do was moan as he lightly brushed my arm taking it off, and while he was kissing my neck and gently nibbling my ears. *Welcome back to heaven, Liz.*

"Will, are you sure no one is going to see us?"

"Yes, it is just us, I promise," I knew then this would forever be one of my favorite vineyards. He pulled me farther into the dense vines of the vineyard.

He was peeling off my clothes. "I can't get enough of you, Lisette. You would be amazed at how often I think of you and of our next time together." We were both feeling flushed at this point, the smells from the vineyard wafting around us were intoxicating. In the air was sweet smells of luscious ripe grapes, thick leaves and foliage, and fresh grass as we lay down in each other's soft embrace. The setting sun would burst through the vines in ebbs and flows as the leaves shifted ever so slightly with the passing breeze. I ran my hand through Will's soft, thick hair as I arched my back as he worked his magic, and I gripped his hair tightly as my senses focused on him.

"Do you like that, Lisette, tell me what you like?" He looked up at me mischievously, I was completely naked, and his broad chest was now bare, showing his perfectly sculpted muscles heaving with each hurried breath. It wasn't my nature to voice what I liked during sex, but I didn't want to disappoint.

His tongue swirled deliciously in circles, the sensation coursing through my veins from the top of my head to the tips of my fingers. He was completely focused on me and my pleasure. He stopped again, looking at me. "What do you want, Lisette, I want you to tell me."

After a deep breath, I whispered, "Keep going, I'm so close, don't stop." It was excruciating for him to tease me, and then stop, my desire growing only to be denied final release. It was like he knew every inch of my body, he was so masterful with his gentle movements, and where and how to place his hands and lips.

"You will learn Lisette, sometimes delayed gratification or denial of pleasure is the best. I have some things I can teach you I think… but for now, I will grant your wish." He kissed me passionately. I let myself get taken with the feeling as sweet relief flowed through me in waves until I thought it wouldn't end, and I may die in excruciating bliss. I slumped down in the grass, exhausted. Will was then face-to-face with me as he leaned over my sprawled body, his arms supporting his weight as he pressed his hips into me. He looked down, and seemed pleased by my expression.

"How do you feel?" he asked, searching my face, but by the way the corners of his mouth were turned up, I could see he already knew the answer.

"Will, that was unreal, I thought I had died and gone to heaven for a second," I lazily responded, and with a contented smile, I looked up at the night sky. This was the second time we had the nothing between the heavens and us as we made love.

"Not a bad appetizer to our main course. Are you ready for more, Lisette?" He grabbed a grape off the closest vine, and bit into it. He lowered his body onto mine, and left me breathless with a smoldering kiss as sweet as the grape left on his lips, leaving me hungry for more.

Biting down on my lower lip, I couldn't believe we were doing this out in the open at a vineyard, of all places. Plus, which was certainly a first for me, there were multiple courses to the sexual evening. I couldn't believe it. Having multiple orgasms during one tryst was also another first. Who was this guy?

"Do you trust me?" Will had me lean up on one elbow as he took my one leg over his shoulder, and had me extend it as far as I could. He then straddled my other leg, and slid into me.

He thrust into my raised leg, resting on his shoulder, and he would bite my leg sending shivers down my spine. My head was thrown backward as I felt the wind, as my hair brushed against my shoulder blades. He was looking up towards the sky, chest heaving, we were in perfect sync with one another until the blissful end when we were both satisfied.

Afterwards, we laid in the soft grass for a while, looking up at the darkened sky, and taking in the smells of the vineyard and the gently sloping hills leading to the water below. Then, aware we were outside of a public venue, half naked in the grass, we started to slowly pull on our clothes. We walked hand and hand back to the vineyard entrance to our special Gold Room.

I felt like I was walking on air, the scenery was gorgeous, the sound of running water from a meticulously decorated fountain added to the surroundings—and I had the sexiest man alive on my arm. Will pulled another grape off the vine for me, and I took in the delicious sweetness. He kissed me lightly. *Grape kisses are the best, yum. I don't think I will ever be able to eat a grape again without thinking of tonight, and I'm okay with such a delicious memory.*

When I grabbed my phone out of my bag to quickly check the time and text Jodi when I thought I might be back at our apartment, my sandal caught one of cobblestones in the walkway. I gasped and immediately felt Wills hand steadying me, but my phone was jarred from my hand, and splashed into the bubbling water fountain nearby.

Without thinking twice, I retrieved my now cracked and dripping phone.

"My phone, oh my gosh! It is ruined. My phone is useless, it's dead, and so are my work emails, contacts, everything."

It is sobering a feeling when you lose your lifeline and connections. Will was stifling laughter, watching me fish out my pathetic-looking phone. He pulled a leaf off of it for me, and looked at me earnestly.

"Don't worry, doll, I can have Max have a brand new one waiting for you first thing tomorrow morning. I will have him sync it with your email, calendar, and will try to retrieve as much contact information as possible." Watching my pained face, he leaned in and kissed my nose.

"It will work out, I promise." He dazzled me with his reassuring smile. I thought back to our passionate moments earlier, and I felt better. When he stepped away as he called Max, I could hear the low murmur of his voice, but couldn't distinguish what he was saying. I felt cared for in the moment, I had a problem and he solved it. This seemed to be a growing trend, and maybe he was right. Have I always attracted this much trouble?

For our candlelight dinner, Will ordered a fantastic wine, and the food was unbelievable. We discussed the account team he was putting together, and he asked my input on those I knew, or people I wanted to add to the team.

"What about Jason? He seems like a focused, driven and goal-oriented talent. Could you add him to the team?" Will asked, as he sipped the full-bodied red wine.

"Jason may be focused and driven, but I have suspicions he may be a little ruthless, too. Let's call it creative differences. I was hoping to bring in Cat instead of Jason, if you don't mind." I watched his reaction. This would be the moment to determine how much *I am* responsible for the building of the team, whether he would override my decision, or let me lead some of the direction. I waited.

"Hmmm, is there anything I should know about him, Lisette?" he asked, one eyebrow raised.

I had to divert my gaze as he leveled me with his intense stare reflecting the flickering of the candlelight. I was starting to feel the wine, and had to be careful. As much as I despised Jason, I think I had him right where I wanted him with his latest screw up, and I didn't want to blow the whole thing open by bringing Will in on all the sordid details. It wouldn't do any good, and I could make more enemies. I had to risk keeping our conversations to myself.

"Nothing I can't handle," I said with a confident smile, and quickly tried to move the conversation to Cat's accomplishments and credentials. To my surprise he agreed to move Cat to the account team, and leave off Jason. I was pleasantly surprised.

After the amazing meal and great conversation, we headed to the parking lot.

"How about you let me drop you at your home, I have a car coming in five minutes." Will grabbed my hand to spin me so I was facing him.

"I have my car here, but thank you for offering, Will." I smiled back sweetly.

He drew his arms around the small of my back, and looked up towards the night sky. "Well, you did just drop your phone in a fountain, which means you would have to drive home without any cell service. I think, to be safe, you should let me drop you. I can have one of the staff pick up your car and drop it off at your place, and you would have it for your drive tomorrow. Plus, after a couple of glasses of wine, it makes sense, Lisette. Let me take care of you." He had a devilish smile, and was gently kissing my neck, making my legs turn to putty.

"You make a compelling argument, Will. I'm a little curious about this staff you mentioned. How many people do you have on your payroll?" True, he makes a lot of money in his current role, but his comment on "staff" made me wonder what type of wealth would allow for a host of extra individuals on the payroll.

"I employ a few people for a couple different reasons. Story for another day perhaps, as here is our ride now." He put his hands in his pockets as a dark limo pulled up. Was there some forethought put into the evening, more than I originally thought? The driver got out and opened the doors.

"Thanks, Doffing, we will be taking Lisette home. I am going to make a quick call, so Lisette can give you the address. Please put up the partition. Lisette, can I have your car keys, please?" Will quietly directed, and then stepped aside to make his phone call. I dug my keys out of my bag and gave them to Will. I sank into the nice leather seats, and gave the directions to Doffing, a man in his forties.

As Will was arranging the pickup of my car, I decided to take this opportunity to find out a little bit more about his personal staff. He had deflected my question earlier, which either meant he didn't feel comfortable sharing this part of his life with me, or didn't want to dig into it for another reason. Part of me felt slightly insulted that he didn't trust me enough to be completely open and honest, but I also knew the nature of our relationship as it stood was primarily physical, and tied in with work. I knew nothing about his family, his personal life outside of our time together, or much else about the elusive past of William Duke. When I Googled him, all that came up was more recent work-related articles and pictures, but missing was any mention of his personal life. Wonder if this means our relationship was intended to be a temporary fling, and if he was intentionally keeping me at bay, preventing me from getting too close to the real him?

"Doffing, it is very nice to meet you. Thank you for picking us up. How long have you worked with William?" I couldn't resist prying, I knew I probably shouldn't, but since William was still on the phone, I used the opportunity.

"Nice to meet you, Miss Lisette. I have entered your address into the GPS so we will be on our way shortly. I have worked with Mr. Duke for several years now, and before that, I was in the employ of Mr. Bradley for fifteen years. Some of us work exclusively with Mr. Duke now, and most of us stay at his lakefront estate in Winnetka."

My breath caught in my throat. When Doffing said the name Mr. Bradley, I couldn't help but wonder if he meant *the* Mr. Bradley from Burke and Bradley ad agency? Of course, it is a common enough name, so it could be a coincidence. He also mentioned a lakefront property in Winnetka, Illinois, known for being the most private and elite suburb of Chicago. Is this the same William Duke we are talking about? Beyond his luxurious condo he has a second home. How would employees who used to work for Mr. Bradley, assuming it is the same Mr. Bradley whose name was on the company sign, then change to work for William Duke? My mind was spinning. This one question had opened up a laundry list of other questions for me. I was about to ask a follow up when

Will opened the car door.

"We are all set, Doffing," Will said briskly, and the partition started to slide shut. I had missed my chance. I didn't want to seem as though I was prying, I am sure Doffing assumed I knew more about "Mr. Duke" than I did, and I didn't want to get him into trouble, so I decided not to mention anything.

"Everything okay, Will?" I asked, noticing his curt tone when he got into the car. "Yeah, I had to take care of some business. Your car will be waiting in front of your place by tomorrow morning, and the keys will be placed on top of the wheel on the driver's side for you to grab them. That way it will be there waiting for you hidden from view, but you don't have to worry about anyone waking you up."

"Thanks for organizing my car delivery." What business has put him in such a mood? His jovial self was replaced with a stoic look.

"Anything I can do to help? You look like you have a lot on your mind," I offered hesitantly. He looked over at me, and something shifted in his eyes. They grew darker, and more intense. I could tell he wanted me, and it made my cheeks flush, and I was feeling flushed at the very thought of him touching me.

His face relaxed a little as he pulled me close in the back of the town car. "Nothing for you to worry about, doll, but unfortunately I do have some business to take care of tonight after we drop you at your place. He was kissing my forehead.

"Yes, yes, absolutely. Sorry you have to return to work, which doesn't sound like any fun at all. Thank you for a wonderful evening though." I peered up at him as he pulled me close. I worried about what was weighing on his mind, but I knew he didn't want me to pry. I was content being close to him for the ride, and was only sorry it had to end.

The office was in busy chaos leading up to the Florida photo shoot. When I arrived at my desk I had a box waiting for me with a card. It was my new phone, and the letter was from Max.

Heard your phone took a bath, hope you enjoy this one. I installed your email and uploaded contacts for you from your last device. I also added a couple apps you may find helpful. One allows you to locate your phone if it is lost or stolen. I use it all the time when I forget which conference room I left it in last. List of passwords attached. Hope you enjoy! –Max

Wow, leave it to Max to go above and beyond. The phone was much more advanced than my last one. I made a mental note to go in and change the passwords at some point, but was thrilled to have a phone again.

I was looking around for Max to thank him, but Blondie and Max were out of the office running continuous errands for the execs. Unfortunately Will's late-night work session led to business out of town, so I was without him for the days leading up to the shoot.

My spirits rose a little once I landed in Florida, taking in the beautiful view and gorgeous weather. I was relieved knowing Will had arrived at the shooting site a little before I did.

All of the gorgeous models we brought in for the shoot noticed Will immediately. He had a great way with anyone we brought in as he described the vision, and the importance he put on their role in displaying our vision. He has a knack for making people feel at ease with him the moment they meet him. This ability unfortunately led to the gorgeous models touching him lightly on the arm as he talked, and draping themselves around him as they became more comfortable. My stomach churned as I noticed their gorgeous hair shimmered as they threw their heads back to laugh at all of his jokes.

I knew it was his job, which he was very good at, and I knew we were not exclusive or anywhere close to dating, but I could feel a knot in my stomach forming. I was jealous, and I hated the jealous feelings that stirred inside me. As if I didn't already doubt myself enough, it had me wondering if he had met these girls before on other shoots, if he had also grabbed drinks with them, and tugged their hair as they made passionate love.

I continued to be painfully aware of how females reacted to him. It was like they had sensors alerting them as soon as someone incredibly masculine and handsome walked into a room. They rotated around him like the way planets rotate around the sun. When we have grabbed drinks or dinner, I noticed it with regular wait staff. However, he had the same impact on super models and models who traveled the world because they were breathtaking enough to make a career out of their beauty—and this took my jealously to new level. Thoughts started breaking in about why he would want someone like me, someone normal, when he could have any one of these extraordinary supermodels who practically drooled all over him. He had the wealth; he had the looks. Perhaps I was more on the defensive because surrounded by co-workers and staff, we couldn't interact like we typically would if we were alone. As far as everyone else was concerned, we were co-workers, and this was how we intended it to stay, so I kept my distance.

I tried to occupy my mind with all the commotion of the shoot, organization of the settings and scenery, and other miscellaneous items I was in charge of for this particular trip. Since I was so new to the team, I didn't have a lot of responsibility, but I took it upon myself to learn from everyone in charge around me. I asked a lot of questions, like how they reached those outcomes, and dug into the creative process and administration process around each detail so at the very least, I would be better equipped with the various knowledge so I could be more useful next time. I tried desperately not to look over at Will, knowing he was dealing with the talent, which seemed the smartest course of action because I would feel the tight knot at the pit of my stomach with every glance over to him. Whenever possible, I tried to be on the opposite side of the room. As I thrust myself into my work, I was luckily able to keep myself focused and busy enough to not dwell on which gorgeous lanky blond bombshell had her arms draped around Will this time. As I approved the lighting for another shoot, I noticed out of the corner of my eye that my bag was vibrating. *Shoot, I should probably carry my phone in case someone needs to reach me.*

Fishing my phone out of my bag, I watched the flash from one of the shoots create a strobe light atmosphere as the photographers moved around the room, taking different shots and changing direction. Their input ranged from "more fierce," to "I need more life in your eyes, energy," and "beautiful, absolutely gorgeous." It was a surreal whirlwind, and I couldn't believe I was there to witness it. It was astounding to see some of my images take form, or be reshaped, based on the creative teams' input. I was living a dream, and felt incredibly lucky. Peeking quickly at my phone, I checked what emails might have flooded in, or texts from family and friends.

There I saw several missed calls from Jodi, so I stepped farther away from the photo shoot trying to find a private spot where I could give her quick call.

"Liz, thank God you're okay. I tried calling you like twenty times!"

"Sorry Jodi, I was away from my phone for a while during the photo shoot, trying to learn as much as I can. What's going on?"

"Liz, this isn't *just any phone call*. I was worried about you because someone broke into our place, they took some of my stuff that was in the TV room area, but they trashed your room, and shredded your stuff with a knife or something. They ruined everything, and cut all your curtains and destroyed your clothes. They busted your computer into a ton of little pieces. Liz, are you there?"

My breath was leaving my lungs and body, and I suddenly couldn't remember how to breathe properly. I felt like I had been dunked in a bath full of ice cubes, or a bucket of ice and snow was thrown on me. The chill of fear and disbelief spread through me like a bad rash. I felt completely isolated and alone, and horribly violated. I looked back vacantly to the shoot, watching another model laughing near Will.

"Liz, are you there? That's not all. They left a note on our kitchen table, and all it said was, "I'm watching you." The cops think this is personal vendetta against you, and they have me staying with my friend Becky, but they want to talk to you. Can you come back?"

Something started to rise in my throat. I stumbled to the back of the building, finding a side exit door. I shoved my way outside, trying to get some air, feeling like I was spinning ever so slightly. I stumbled as the outdoor air hit my face, and in my dismay I hardly noticed my heel catching the ground, causing me to lunge forward until my hands stopped my fall. I slumped to the floor, kneeling on the ground, staring for countless minutes in disbelief at my phone in my hands. Putting the phone on the ground, I tried to steady myself with outreached hands, as if bracing myself against some invisible hurricane wind threatening to blow away every ounce of me. I clicked the red button on my phone to hang up. I couldn't speak, I couldn't think, I realized I wasn't breathing, and could feel my chest starting to heave as it fought for breath. Then...I felt a strong hand on my shoulder.

Luckily no one else was around as Will crouched over next to me. "Lisette, are you okay? Do you feel ill, what's wrong?" He lifted me gently from my knees, supporting my weight as I barely managed to look him in the eyes. He must have noticed something written in my expression, so he cupped my face in his hands and brought his face closer to mine. His pained gaze finally cut through the dense fog I was in to reach me, "Lisette, talk to me," his voice commanded. Desperately searching my eyes, I could feel myself coming back from miles away.

"My place, someone broke into my place, but they didn't target Jodi. I was the target, they... they destroyed everything.

Everything… and left a note saying they are watching. The police want to talk to me, they got everything Will… nothing is left… Will, they were in my *home*." I bent over, putting my hands on my knees to steady myself. The realization of my words suddenly sinking in, I could feel myself starting to gasp for breaths. I was hyperventilating. Will wrapped me in a reassuring hug as he whispered in my ear.

"You're okay, doll. You're going to be fine. I'm here with you, and nothing bad is going to happen, okay? Breathe, Lisette, just breathe. That's my girl," Will said in a calm, controlled voice.

The next several moments were a blur, but I somehow ended up with a bag in my hands to breathe into, and Max and Will talking in hushed tones. The two of them were lifesavers. Before I knew it, they had booked me a flight so I could go home to discuss the destruction of my property and the threatening note with the cops. Max came up with a plausible cover story for me having to leave the photo shoot on such short notice so the other account team members wouldn't wonder why I was flaking on them, while there was work to be done, without divulging this personal horror show. They also arranged transit for me, as I sat in a stunned daze, so I could hurry back to the hotel to pack my bags. I normally enjoy sorting everything so it fits perfectly in my suitcase, but this time I found no joy in the process as I fought back stunned tears and stuffed wrinkled clothing into my suitcase.

Back at the hotel, I couldn't help but feel sorry for myself, I thought I finally hit a stroke of luck— landing such a great advertising gig, an amazing spot running my own ad campaign for a huge client, being able to travel, while meeting new people and living the dream—and meeting a person like Will. Now I had to risk it all by leaving a shoot suddenly due to a ridiculous personal issue. Leaving my own photo shoot, for a competition I won, with a team I helped put together. I couldn't oversee any of the creative pieces, and was forced to come up with a cover story to hopefully protect my reputation. I had to leave the sexiest man on earth with a room full of supermodels instead of having a secret candlelight dinner with him on the beach. I fought back the tears at how unfair it all seemed. I couldn't let myself sink into a depression on top of everything else. I heard a knock at the door. Looking through the peephole, I saw Will.

He was leaning against the wall looking at me. "How are you holding up? May I come in?" I nodded, and let him in as I tried to compose myself so I did not let on how rattled I was.

"Lisette, are you on the next flight?" I nodded. Concerned, he cleared his throat. "I think I should go with you Lisette, you shouldn't be alone right now."

"No, it would only raise suspicion with everyone here at the shoot if you left, too. I will be fine, the police want to talk to me, and I'm sure they will be with me at my place as I look through the damage. It will be long process, and

183

lots of paperwork and questions to be answered. Honestly, I would feel better if you stayed. I feel bad enough leaving Florida in the middle of the photo shoot. Please make sure everyone knows with this fake emergency Max has created that I regretfully had to leave, I don't want them to think I'm ditching my job for no reason." My eyes pleaded, but I couldn't handle him coming back with me, all the questions the others would have, and everything else I have to face back home.

He shoved his hands deep in his pockets and nodded. "If this is what you want. I have no choice but to stay. Text me once you have a chance to connect with the police, let me know if they have any leads. If you need anything, don't hesitate to ask, okay? You may have won this one, but you can't stop me from worrying about you. Stay in close communication so I know you're safe." His was adamant, and had a dangerous dark look in his eyes. Fighting back tears was so hard when as he looked at me in his certain way.

"Hey, it is going to be okay, all right?" He came in close, and wrapped me in another big, strong, assuring hug. "Can I see a little smile from you before I go?" I sighed and played with my thumb ring, feeling overwhelmed.

"How about this? How did I find out my dad was a construction-site thief?" Will was holding one of my hands, and I couldn't help but smile a little.

"I don't know, how?"

"Well, I didn't know my dad was a construction site thief at first, but when I got home all the signs were there." He flashed me a big pleased-with-himself grin, and I couldn't help but smile.

"Okay, yeah, yeah, you know you're crazy. Now I have to finish here and head to the airport. Thanks for coming over Will, I really appreciate it." Will kissed me lightly on my forehead, and I walked him to the door. It was incredibly hard to see him walk down the hallway, as I spiraled into my own internal hell as I wondered what horror waited for me back home. I knew I had to make him stay for it was the right thing to do, even though I wanted nothing more than to curl up with him, and hide under a mountain of blankets, forgetting the outside world. I had no such luxury, and didn't have the time to bathe in self-pity.

The real world was dragging me down from the clouds, and from my recently charmed existence. The room felt cold without Will there as I finished my packing. My hands were shaking, and I realized how quickly I went from being ecstatic about everything in my life to feeling like I was slowly drowning.

CHAPTER 16

O nce in the cab, I watched the trees roll by as the cabbie started to drive me towards my apartment. It didn't feel like I was going home, it didn't feel like home now, and the police cars outside my place certainly didn't help the feeling. I had called the officer in charge whose name Jodi gave me, to let him know I was coming back so they could meet me at the scene of the crime. I took a deep breath as I paid the cab driver, bracing myself for what would inevitably be a trying next couple of hours.

My luggage was left on the driveway as I was ushered to a plain-clothes officer by the door. They took me through my place, asking me questions as I surveyed the damage. My tongue felt thick, I could barely form words as I felt like I was talking through a mouthful of gelatin. Everything seemed to take longer and be more difficult as we waded through my destroyed belongings—and the police's prying questions.

In my room, I realized I hardly had anything left. They took the time to cut up most of my clothes, my furniture was ruined, desk and dresser drawers were opened and the contents thrown about. It looked like a tornado had unleashed its fury over every square inch of my room, while Jodi's belongings were miraculously untouched.

After getting the police officer's blessing to take with me what remaining clothes I had, I also gathered some of Jodi's clothing she told me I could take to help get me through the next couple weeks. I wasn't going to stay here, and I would ultimately be living out of a suitcase for a while.

While emptying one of my shattered drawers, I noticed the cards I had received from both Phil Burns for the flowers, and William Duke for the picture frame, were missing. They were the only personal items I noticed were taken, but I didn't mention it to the police because I thought it would only open another can of worms, and mean more questions. Because my money and few pieces of jewelry remained, the police thought the break-in was intended to send a message—*I was being watched*, and someone might want to do me harm. We had no leads though, and I couldn't point them in any directions as to who could possibly want to stalk me.

Exhausted after a long day with the police, they finally released me to go to a hotel, where I texted Will.

I'm fine, staying at the Radisson downtown. Hope all is good with the photo shoot. – Liz

Yes, it sounded curt, and a little unlike me, but I was too exhausted and emotionally drained to think straight, let alone care. Will texted me a couple photos from the shoot, which made me feel worse instead of better, so I shut my phone off for the night, and decided to go to bed early. I hoped a new day would put me in better spirits.

The police made it clear they didn't want me staying at my place for a while, so I was beholden to my friends for the next couple days, bouncing around to different apartments when it made sense, or staying at hotels. I was also putting in a lot of hours at work to keep my mind off what I was missing in Florida. When Will arrived back midday he called me into his office as soon as he returned.

I knew I would field a lot of questions regarding where I had rested my head the last few days.

I was met by scrutiny as Will dug into my suitcase lifestyle for the past couple days.

"It honestly is fine Will, my friends are being very gracious, and letting me live like a nomad with them for the time being. It is a little tedious, and I can't take advantage of their hospitality for too long, but I can make it work for a while." I struggled to produce a smile.

"It can't be easy, and what do you plan to do once the police allow you back in your place?" Will was sitting on the edge of his desk, arms folded as I sat in one of his office chairs.

"I'm guessing I will go back there. Maybe invest in some better locks or some sort of security system. I haven't thought very far ahead to be honest. I'm hoping they will catch the crazy homeless person who decided to have some fun in our apartment." I was still trying to convince myself this had *nothing* to do with me personally.

Will was leveling me with his gaze, and started pacing the office. "I have thought about this in Florida, and on the trip back, and I think I have a solution. I want you to stay with me, Lisette, at my place. You will have your own room, your own space, until this whole thing blows over, and they catch the person who for some reason has decided to fixate on you. I travel a lot, as you know, you would have the place to yourself, but my building is incredibly secure with a state-of-the-art protection system. My place also has its own security system, so I know you would be safe. I have plenty of room, so you won't be imposing." He paused and studied my face, waiting for a response.

I gulped at the prospect. *Stay with Will, at his place?* I couldn't believe what he was suggesting; the thought had never crossed my mind.

"Will, the offer is so incredibly gracious, but I can't stay with you. We hardly know each other, I mean, we are getting to know each other, but you don't know me all that well, nor I know you. Moving in with someone, even temporarily, is a big deal. I couldn't impose. I will figure out something, plus what are the chances they would come back?" I hoped my own words would help reassure me, but I wasn't so sure.

My mind was racing, and I was trying to convince myself that this was an isolated incident—that the destruction was random, and I would be perfectly fine. If I absolutely had to, I could go back to the apartment. I felt like I had just watched a marathon of frightening movies, the one where the scary goon is lurking somewhere outside the window, and he calls to say he is outside watching you. Except once the movie ends, I can retreat to my room, knowing it was all done for entertainment value—a fictional situation to make you jump out of your seat. However... this was my life, and no matter how many times I squeezed my eyes shut, and then opened them again, I was still in this horror movie, and whoever was watching me could be around any corner.

Unfortunately, the list of friends was short for those I could impose on for a temporary living situation beyond a couple days here and there. With Jodi already staying with Becky, no one was left. I didn't have family close by, and I had a job I had to think about downtown. Life doesn't' stop because someone smashes up your space, and ruins your personal privacy.

Will looked like I had slapped him across the face. "Lisette, you can't be serious. No way you're going back there, let alone stay there after all of this. If they broke in once, they can do it again, and this time you could be there. It's not going to happen, sorry. I won't allow it, it would be crazy for me to let you walk out of here, and go back there." Exasperated, he ran a hand through his hair.

"Lisette, you're going to stay with me, and I'm going to tell you why. Sure, I don't know you like the boy who grew up next door might know you, but when do we ever really know someone? Friends betray each other, married couples cheat and get divorced, family can disappoint you and let you down, and guys you're seeing can turn out to be jerks. But a good indicator of someone's character is what he does when it really counts, when the pressure is on, and you're in a moment of crisis or struggle. What counts is when you really need that friend, family member, or new guy to come through for you and help. It is those moments, when it is not easy or convenient, when you're able to truly measure the man." It was hard to concentrate on his words when I felt like his eyes were peeling back every inch of my resolve. He took a deep breath and continued, moving closer to me.

"In my mind, this is all you need to know, because I am someone you can rely on when life gets tough. I know you don't know me that well, but I care about you. I feel like I have been cut open, knowing someone bad is looking for you, and imagining what could have happened if you were there, and I think the only cure for such a feeling is making sure I do whatever I can to protect you. All I can think about is knowing you will be safe with me, so please. I promise this is not a ploy to get you to myself, and you can even have your own space. I honestly need you in a place I know you will be safe, and my building's security system is beyond reproach." While I was again playing with my thumb ring, a number of thoughts went through my head. I couldn't believe I was in this spot, talk about a relationship killer, forcing a guy to take me in like I was a stray.

"Will, honestly, this is too much to ask of you." I sucked in a shaky breath, taking in his tall physique, those strong shoulders, his pleading eyes, and his Superman strength as he pulled me in for a deep hug. My willpower was weakening with each passing second in his warm embrace. It felt so good to have someone looking out for me, being concerned about my well being beyond the niceties of everyday pleasantries. Of course, this situation was far from everyday "normal."

His deep voice, heavy with emotion, pleaded, "Let me do this for you, Lisette. No one at the office has to know, I promise. We may need to tell Max, but we can trust him. The question is, do you trust me?" He was leveling me with his intense gaze. His arms, shoulders, and face looked tense, and I could tell he was consciously forcing his limbs to relax as he searched my face, waiting for my response. I was distracted by his look— concerned and pleading, determined and unbending. I was racking my brain for some reason, some other plausible excuse to avoid this situation. It was crazy to think of moving into the mansion he called home. I couldn't believe I was considering it. I saw a million ways this could end badly, but couldn't articulate any of them because he was wearing me down.

Running a shaking hand through my hair, "Will, I…." and I couldn't finish the sentence. Will took my trembling hand in his, and with his other hand placed it on the side of my face. His hand rested around my neck, peering down at me. He placed my hand on his chest, his hand covering mine, I could feel his heart racing.

"Lisette, feel my heart, it is racing because I would never forgive myself if something happened to you, and I'm terrified you are going to turn me down. Let me protect you. Come on, don't make me regret paying a disgusting amount of money for a top-of-the-line security system when I don't get to use it when it counts. I need to get my money's worth on this, don't I?" His hopeful smile melted me, and I couldn't fight against it anymore. *Was he this afraid for me?*

Okay, maybe I could stay at his highly-secured, heavily guarded place for a short while because it is a safe. I was sure they would quickly find the crazy person who threatened me, and then we would go back to normal life. I was still trembling, overwhelmed with the whole situation, and slightly terrified of the hold he had on my psyche. Being putty in his hands, I knew moving in with him would probably drop me down farther into this rabbit hole.

Liz, don't fall for this man, because people like him don't fall for people like me. It is only a matter of time before he goes back to his supermodels and fast living. Convinced this was a temporary situation, I was worried if I got in too deep, I wouldn't be able to survive the outcome. I was afraid I might lose myself to him. This could be the guy to ruin me for all other guys, forever, but I couldn't see myself confessing this hidden concern directly with him anytime soon.

The last thing any guy wants to hear is the "relationship" talk, and I refused to be the girl who asked too much too early in a relationship. I kept telling myself: I knew going into this with Will, it would only be a fling, if I'm being reasonable with myself. I didn't expect to find such a great guy, the whole package and then some, a man unlike any I had ever met or thought existed. Hell, he is offering me solace in a place where I can sleep without freaking out that a crazy person is hovering over my bed. I guess I would be crazy to say no?

"Okay Will, if you're sure," I responded meekly, feeling the loss of more than my heart to this man with each passing moment.

He studied my face, as if reading my mind. "I don't make big decisions without being sure, and this was an easy decision," he said, and with a confident smile he pulled me in for a kiss. Our lips melting together, it was a delicious sensation. His kiss made all of my troubles fade to black, as I floated away with him in the moment.

One thing was for sure—in my personal life, my private life, and my romantic life—I was in real trouble.

Jodi's screaming voice on the other end of the phone almost made me drop my coffee.

"So you're saying somehow through all of this, you got an invite to stay at Superman's house, and I'm stuck with Becky? Are you kidding me, you have all the luck." Jodi was caught off guard when I told her about the recent turn of events.

"Yeah, I don't know Jodi. Talk about making a sticky situation even stickier. We have this covert cover-up thing going where he is going to pick me up from my friends place with my duffle bag of clothes for the week, and go over to his place after work. This way we can both leave the office at different times so no one notices. Eventually this whole this is going to boil over because normal people like me can't keep secrets like this for long, ugh, I just don't know." I toyed with my thumb ring, and was hoping Jodi could assure me I wasn't making a huge mistake.

"Well, wait a second, Liz. I think you could keep a charade like this going for a quite a while, if you ask me. Hey, I got to run, things are getting busy in the store, but let me know how it goes once you get settled. You are one lucky girl."

It didn't make me feel any better when I learned some of the supermodels from the Florida shoot were back in the Chicago office, and in Will's office specifically, going over the pictures, and what needed to be reshot in one of our studios. Since I was running point on the Prescott Pine collection, I was up on the executive level, watching the girls, whose short, tight skirts hardly covered their asses, prance around the water cooler.

Will motioned to one of them to come to his office, and shut the door. I felt like a creep, but I couldn't help stealing a couple glances through the open shades of his office windows. She was leaning over his desk, undoubtedly showing some cleavage, as they talked animatedly. Then I saw it, he came around the desk and gave her a hug, and a quick kiss on the cheek.

Gulp, he kissed the beautiful supermodel, yes, it was on the cheek, but buddies don't kiss on the cheek. Only people involved kiss, and he also hugged her. I think I'm going to be sick. Wait a second, Liz, you didn't make any promises, neither of you gave up the right to date or see other people.

Gag, but a supermodel? Seriously Will? He can't date someone normal looking? Oh, do you mean like you Liz? Maybe he is sick of normal, and wants something a little more extraordinary. He probably feels sorry for me, for my stuff getting ruined, so he is offering a place to stay because it's the chivalrous thing to do. Maybe he is a playboy, despite what he said, but at least he is a chivalrous playboy. Ugh, either way this is not looking good for you, Liz. Kiss your Superman goodbye.

After the display in his office with a lanky blond model, I could hardly think straight, but luckily everyone was running in and out of rooms, too busy with photos and designs to notice my slack-jawed, pale expression of rebuff on my face. I felt like I was a frozen statue, rooted in one place, unable to move after what I witnessed, and I also felt a little cheap—although I knew I didn't have the right to feel betrayed.

True, no promises were made, no definitions behind what this steamy thing between us was or is. More like was. Stop standing here like a dazed fool, Liz, you've got to get out of here and clear your head.

It was close enough to the lunch hour where I could bail and get some much-needed R&R at the store Jodi managed. I needed someone to talk to—and something amazing to wear tonight when Will picks me up. Although I felt brutally rejected, and wiser to the fact he was obviously dating other women, I could still look damn good while feeling sorry for myself. He couldn't take that away from me.

As I pulled into the ramp across the street from Jodi's new job as a store manager, I noticed a shabby red pickup pull in behind me. *Didn't Jodi mention something about a red truck outside our place? She thought he looked like the creep from the bar. Could this be the same guy? You're getting paranoid again Lizzie, and now is not the time to have a full-on psychological breakdown.*

As I drove up the ramp, I kept looking in my review mirror to see the driver's face, but the person was wearing a hat and shades, which made it difficult to determine if it were a man or woman. Once I turned a corner, I tried to quickly drive up the next segment of ramp so I could maneuver my car into a spot near the steps to hopefully get out of my car before the driver had a chance to park. I decided I couldn't be too cautious.

Heart pounding, I floored my vehicle and whirled it around the next corner, luckily finding an open spot close enough to the stairs. Typically I would check the mirror, and nonchalantly grab my bag as I got out of my vehicle, but this time I couldn't whip my seatbelt off fast enough and fly towards the stairs. To my horror, I could hear the truck park behind me, and a door slam. I started booking it down flights as fast as my legs could carry me. Someone was in the stairwell with me because I could hear the clanging of the handrail as he started jumping down the stairs. It must be a guy, to jump down the stairs with such force, and I could hear his boots hitting the ground as the familiar thud of rubber soles on cement became louder. I had a choice to either run across the street, or hide behind a row of large metal garbage cans against the side of the stairwell—and hope he walks by me.

I hid behind the garbage cans so he couldn't follow me into Jodi's work, crouched low behind one bin, and held my breath. His footsteps paused at the end of the stairs, and then walked off in the other direction. My heart was pounding in my ears. I quietly peeked out from behind the cans, and saw him disappear into a row of stores down the block. From the back, I couldn't tell who it was, his collar was drawn up, and the baseball hat covered his hair. However, seeing him go into a store made me feel slightly foolish, because if someone was following me, would he pretend to go shopping? I wasn't sure, but when I gathered the courage enough to cross the street towards Jodi's store, my heart was in my throat, and I practically ran into her store.

"Hey, lady, thanks for dropping in to my second casa. Whew, you smell kind of weird." Jodi was thumbing through some of the racks when I came in, and she gave me a big hug.

"Yeah, I was over by the garbage cans back there for a second, long story." I hoped she wouldn't press the issue. I was busy convincing myself I was nuts for thinking someone could be following me, especially with how many red trucks are driving around town, and the last thing I needed was Jodi also freaking out.

Jodi started haphazardly spraying me with various perfumes as I walked around looking at her new collection.

As we walked through the store, I filled her in on what I had witnessed at the office.

"So you need a certain kind of dress so he'll never want to look at another supermodel again, right? I think I have a couple of those on hand." Jodi was smiling to herself as she pulled off various dresses and designer-looking outfits, adding to the already overflowing bundles of fabric draped over her arm for me.

"It wasn't because he was looking at her Jodi, come on. I mean in his line of work, and with the people he knows, that is purely ridiculous. I was caught off guard with the hug and kiss is all. They could have at least had the decency to pull down the shade." I was becoming crabbier by the second as I rehashed the whole ordeal.

"Yeah, then they would have done more than only hug and kiss. Think of it as him doing you a favor, this way you know where you stand, and you won't get attached. This is a gift Liz, embrace it." Jodi set up all of her selections in a spacious fitting room in the back.

"A gift, what gift exactly are you referring to that William supposedly gave me, while making me feel like shit at the office?" I could feel my bottom lip poke out in a bit of a pout. *Yeah, so I'm being a total baby right now. Is there a better time or place to be a complete baby without fear of judgment than with your best friend at her new amazing store during a retail therapy session? I think not! Having the store practically to yourself, while you complain and dish about guys, is every single girl's ideal day, so for crying out loud, give yourself a break, Liz!*

"It's easy, Liz, he gave you the gift of no-strings-attached mind-blowing sex with a guy who could be Clark Kent's gorgeous brother, with none of the messy relationship consequences. You're living the dream, girlfriend." Jodi gave me a smug I-wish-I-was-you smile as she shut the door to the dressing room. I made myself busy trying to squeeze into a number of the crazy items she brought me to try on. The first dress looked like someone had painted the fabric on me it was so tight. *Eeek, chin up, Liz, you don't have to like all of them, you only need one.*

This was Jodi's idea of a best-case-scenario type of situation with Will, but I wasn't like Jodi. *Maybe I need to change my mindset, I should be a little more carefree, and let the whole situation work itself out. Yeah, it doesn't matter if he is seeing other girls on the side, because I can see other guys, too. You're free, single, and not tied down, maybe it is time you started acting like it, Liz.*

I went through a dozen outfits that all made me feel less than fabulous, finally one stood out. It was a halter dress in a perfect shade of green to really accentuate my dark eyes and hair, flattering in all the right places, and enhancing to my figure, and the one I received the appropriate amount of compliments from Jodi and the other sales clerk. Plus, they both told me I would be nuts if I didn't buy it. Once I got beyond the sticker shock, I thought it wouldn't be the worst thing in the world if I splurged a bit once in a while.

"Liz, you are a knockout. You could stand to gain a few pounds in a couple areas, but if he can peel his eyes away from you for one second when you're in this dress, I will be surprised. If this dress doesn't empower you tonight when he picks you up, I don't know what will. Remember though; stay aloof and independent. Tell him you had been out having drinks with a friend, and leave it vague. It will drive him nuts." Jodi gushed on as she had me twirl in my new dress. I wasn't sure if taking advice from Jodi on this one was a good idea, but after the bizarre turn of events this morning in the office, I was ready to try a new approach for my own sanity.

After paying, and hoping I wouldn't receive a fraud-prevention call from my bank at the ludicrous amount I just dropped on one dress, I hugged Jodi and quickly made my way across the street. Clutching my bag tightly as I went back up the stairs, I noticed the red truck was nowhere to be seen, much to my relief.

The rest of the day flew by, and since I was back at my desk working on copy for the Prescott Pine ad campaign, I didn't have to run into Will or any scantily clad women the rest of the day. After work, I rushed to my friend's place to change into the dress, and prepare my bags for when Will picked me up later. Seven o'clock couldn't come fast enough.

Will held the car door open for me, and placed my bags in the trunk. I could see him checking me out in my new dress.

"You're looking amazing tonight, Lisette. Green is definitely your color." He gave me a cockeyed grin, and I pushed down some venomous words now rising in response, and reminded myself not to be so jealous.

"I had a couple drinks with a friend, and didn't have a chance to change. Thanks for the compliment, though." As I slid into the front seat of his fancy sports car, I should have guessed he would drive something fast and expensive.

"Liz, your new dress is a keeper. Drinks with a friend, huh?

How was it?" He was starting to pry as we pulled out of the parking lot. *Play it cool, be elusive, and start acting like you have a life outside work.*

"Yep, drinks with a friend. It *was fine*, thank you."

"You seem a little tense. Was drinks with your friend okay, or did something happen? Want to talk about it?" I could see the muscles in his jaw moving, my elusive answers were getting to him.

"No, no, nothing like that. Nothing to talk about really, it was just drinks, and you know, nothing special. I appreciate you taking me in for a few days, please don't think I'm not grateful, but what we do in our personal time is personal, don't you agree? Wasn't that the deal?" I turned towards him in the seat and smiled, looking more innocent and nonchalant than I felt. He was looking a little more furious than I expected.

"You're absolutely correct, Lisette, my bad. We are not each other's keeper, and your personal life is nothing I should pry into," he said through clenched teeth. We drove in tense silence the rest of the way to his place.

As he showed me around what was to be my own space and bathroom for as long as I was his guest, he quickly excused himself to continue working in his study. This left me to my own devices as I started unpacking some of my belongings.

I changed into my dark yoga pants and a soft tank top, and wrapped myself under as many blankets as possible to feel cozy and protected. Despite the cave of blankets I had made,

I still felt skittish and paranoid as the clocked ticked loudly in the silence in my room. How did I feel about this whole "have your own room, I'm not trying to come on to you" thing? Quickly I was sinking into my own horrible thoughts of what some unknown stalker was doing at this very second. I tossed and turned for what seemed like hours, finally taking some herbal sleeping aids in the hopes it would bring the blessed release of sleep to me sooner rather than later. Falling into a fitful sleep, I went into a demented dreamland.

In my dream fog, I found myself running down a deserted road. I sensed an uncomfortable vague feeling I sometimes have in dreams, where I am somewhat aware of the fact I'm not in reality—but along with that foresight also comes a foreboding sensation that something bad is waiting around the corner. I was running down this deserted two-lane highway, with nothing but endless cornfields on either side.

I knew, or sensed, I'd come to a fork in the road, but felt strongly that both paths held impending doom. In my dream I raced up to the fork, propelled by some unknown force, feeling like I had to reach the end of the road. I was trying to find anyone who could help me, but I was alone for the time being. Pausing at the fork, both roads led into dark woods. Behind me were only cornfields, and waiting ahead were dark, dense trees. Turning around, I looked to see if I could go back, but a terrifying twister of red dust was kicking up behind me in the distance. It was taking out the highway and the cornfields as it picked up speed, and my heart sank as I realized I had to keep running, otherwise the dust would eat me alive.

Both paths looked horribly dark and foreboding, which made the decision difficult. I chose the path to the left, and ran into the menacing woods, but I could feel something dark and sinister waiting for me. I was crying as I was running, waiting for the darkness to show itself, when the wooded path turned into stairs—huge descending stairs, and I was falling down them into a dark pit. Tumbling into the darkness, I fell through a hole in the staircase, and spiraled deep into the hidden dungeon. I would never be found there—I was in a place of forgetting. The dark black soil of the surrounding walls started to morph into hands, and the hands were forming into horrible hideous creatures with mouths open, screaming, "We are watching *youuu*." Screaming it over and over, until with shuddering sobs, I bolted upright in my bed with a scream. The momentum of the dream caused me to jump off the bed, and the adrenaline carried me into the far corner of the room where I finally slumped into the fetal position.

Will knocked lightly, came in, and saw me hunched in the corner of the room. He crouched next to me, and gently lifted my face to his.

"Lisette, are you okay? I think you had a nightmare, but it is over now. It is all over, hey, hey, you're going to be okay." His eyes searched mine, as he helped me to my feet.

"I'm sorry I woke you, I think I woke from a horrible dream, and being in new surroundings, I ended up over here. I'm, I'm so embarrassed I don't know what to say." I was still shaking slightly from the dream, a high energy continued coursing through my body.

"You're trembling again, oh sweetie, I'm sorry. Come here." Will pulled me in for a warm, loving bear hug, and I sighed as I leaned into him. My eyes clamped tightly shut as I let myself become completely entwined with him.

"Would you like to stay in my room tonight? It might help you sleep better, and you may feel safer. Plus I'm a great cuddle buddy." Will rewarded me with a boyish, carefree smile.

"Are you sure? I mean, I'm already imposing staying here, and then to encroach on your personal space. I hope you're not doing all of this just to be a nice guy. Are you fine with everything?"

"Lisette, you have to stop thinking and asking, okay? I wouldn't have invited you here if that wasn't the case, and I wouldn't offer if I weren't fine with it. Come on, I have a great California king-sized bed with silk sheets. You're going to love it." He winked, and I acquiesced and followed him down the hall to his room.

CHAPTER 17

Walking by Cat's desk, I stopped in my tracks at the sight of the gorgeous artwork in her ad layouts for the Kramer account, which was a new high-rise luxury shopping center and loft rentals. Being built in the heart of the downtown area would guarantee success-driven city lovers as tenants—those who would kill to live in the heart of a bustling city, and experience high-end shopping conveniently close.

"Cat, your designs are amazing, can you show me your pitch? What are you tasked with for the Kramer account so far?" Ogling her work, I was envious of the fact she is so bloody talented, and it seemed to come effortlessly and easy for her.

She started taking me through her designs and layout, showing me one of the best concepts I had seen.

"Liz, I may be getting a little ahead of myself, but my account team is simply throwing around ideas at this point, and I am hoping to pitch this portfolio the next session. I heard Phil Burns might also stop in at some point to weigh in. This is one of his pet projects. Not sure if they will like it, but I felt inspired so I wanted to put a plan together I feel makes sense, and see what they think. Thanks for the kind words though, Liz, I appreciate it!" She was grinning broadly as I continued to fawn over every inch of her proposal.

"Are you kidding, Cat, with these designs, the team would be crazy to turn down any of these ideas. I think you are really onto something." As I dug into one of the pieces of copy, I felt an ominous presence over my shoulder, and turned to find the smug-looking Jason.

"What are you ladies up to today? Ah, the new Kramer account. A lot of people are vying to get onto that account team, myself included. What makes you think you stand a chance? Are these your ideas, Cat, or did Liz drag you into trying for this so you can both pretend to have corner offices on the exec floor? Didn't I see you up there the other day Liz, were you lost or what?" He looked sickeningly pleased with himself, and uninvited, he started to rifle through some of Cat's designs on her desk.

Cat looked like at any moment, steam would come out of her ears. With her moment of hesitation, I said, "Jason, I was on the exec floor working on the Prescott Pine account, as you know. Why don't you go and bother some other people for a change, can't you see we are working here?" I crossed my arms and waited patiently for him to turn around and leave before things escalated, but I wasn't so lucky.

Jason picked up another piece of Cat's copy, and she snapped, "Look Jason, I better not catch you sneaking around my desk looking at my designs. I trust you as far as I can throw you, which isn't very far. Can you leave us alone now, please?" She started pulling documents out of his slimy grasp, and putting everything back in her folder, while he stood there looking haughty. Once he slinked out of view, Cat also shared a thrilling new proposal with me.

"You know I spin at the Falcon? Charity week is coming up for the restaurants and bars downtown, and I proposed the Falcon as the event site for a charity evening for Burke and Bradley, and Phil Burns *approved it*. The email should be coming out shortly for this Friday's event. He was so pleased with the request, they bought out the Falcon for the whole evening exclusively for Burke and Bradley employees, and I will be spinning at the event. Can you believe it! It is great PR not only for our company, but also for the Falcon. Sounds like a lot of the execs are going, and reporters will be there adding coverage. Isn't that great! They might put my name in the email announcement, so I'm pretty stoked, but getting a bit nervous." Cat was bubbling and brimming with excitement, and I couldn't blame her.

"What amazing news Cat, *good for you*. You absolutely deserve the notoriety, and taking on such a big event task like a charity event for the company, in addition to everything else you have going on, is incredible. I will absolutely be there, and let me know I can help with anything. Sorry about Jason. I would never have asked to look at your copy and design ideas if I knew he would slink up, and try to get a bit of the action." I winced at the memory of Cat's steamed face as Jason got his grubby paws on all of her hard-thought-out pieces.

"Don't worry about it, Jason is Jason, and he'll never change. I figure if I keep doing what I'm doing in the proper way, it is bound to get me noticed, as opposed to taking the easy way all of the time like Jason does. Confidentially, since he has moved up to the executive floor, he hasn't produced a lot of headlining ideas—not since he borrowed and stole his way up there. He's plotting something, but I don't know what. Rumor is that is he is itching to get an interview for this new executive opening on Phil's team. Phil loves him, but lately Jason hasn't brought a lot of new ideas to the table, so I think he is starting to feel a little cornered. However, when he does, Jason starts to scheme and get nasty. Liz, I better get back to it. I have a lot to do before the event. Could you do me a huge favor and proof some of my ideas for the Kramer account? I want to propose them end of week, and could use some new eyes, if you don't mind." Cat's eyes pleaded as she put her hands together in a mock prayer, hoping I would agree.

"Oh my gosh, of course. I would love to take a look and proof your ideas. They look absolutely gorgeous, so I'm sure there won't be a lot of edits to make, but I am happy to jump in and take a look wherever you need me. I'm thrilled you thought of me." Cat squealed in delight and handed me her thick folder to get started. This is what I loved about my job, there was always something new and exciting to dive into. Luckily for me, the majority of what I got paid to do involved creativity and beauty, and when it meant helping out a friend like Cat, it didn't seem like work at all.

CHAPTER 18

The week flew by, and before we knew it, the charity event was here, and all the eager Burke and Bradley employees left to join the executives to support this good cause. Cat looked like a rock star spinning at the Falcon. She was incredibly talented, and eventually as the evening progressed, the whole dance floor was packed, and the drinks were flowing. If nothing else good came of working from Burke and Bradley, at least I found a new friend in Cat. I waved at her when Dustin and I walked in, and she waved back as she bounced to the music.

I scanned the room as we started to walk through the crowds to find the work group. It was incredibly generous of the company to rent out the Falcon for the charity event, which worked out fine for me because it gave my superman a reason to be there, which means I could at least drool over him from afar. I felt better about the whole situation with him after my horrific nightmare, and the way he helped me through a bit of paranoia. I was in a better place emotionally regarding what I was expecting from the situation, which brought me back to my overall giddiness when I ran into him at work functions. Knowing I expected nothing from our current status brought me back to the fun, flirty stage where I could enjoy from the rush that accompanied the chase. Besides, I didn't want to let the thought of him dating other girls impact me.

It was important no one suspected anything between us, in order to avoid the resulting chaos if colleagues knew. It was kind of fun to be in the same room with him, pretending like we have no background whatsoever, while carrying around our delicious little secret. It being slightly taboo, I liked the feeling the innocent danger brought into my life. *I can be a sucker for a little danger every now and then.*

I was surprised to see that Phil and Will were already at the party, near a table where people could bid on the silent auction prizes, all of which benefited charity. Phil was talking with Jason, and waved to us when we walked in. Jason was nodding eagerly, eating a handful of peanuts from the bar, and holding a glass of bourbon in the other hand. He completely ignored Dustin and me.

Phil patted Jason on the shoulder and strode over to us. At the same time, Superman turned, eyeing me from a distance. His face showed no hint of a smile, and in the low-light atmosphere of the bar, he looked dark and foreboding. Judging by his defensive stance and intense gaze, I don't think he appreciated Phil meandering our way, but he stayed by the same table instead of stopping Phil.

"Let me buy you two a drink." Phil crooned over the loud music, as he moved us to the opposite end of the bar from Will.

"I was just chatting with Jason, and he was sharing his wonderful new ideas for the Kramer account. I think we are going to see big things from him in the future." Phil beamed at us as he placed a drink order.

"Oh yeah, what types of ideas did he share with you, Phil?" I asked nonchalantly, hoping this time, I was wrong about Jason. Phil started reciting almost verbatim what Cat had showed us days before. Dustin's eyes widened as he realized Cat created every single detail—not Jason. Jason stole each of her ideas, and tried pawning it off to Phil as his own before Cat could even submit her folder to the account group. Jason was trying to put her in a situation where it would be her word against his.

Bile was rising in my throat at Phil's words. Maybe it was the extra tall glass of wine I had before I came, maybe it was Dustin's bemused expression as he raised both his eyebrows to the ceiling when he heard Phil mention Jason, maybe it was how happy and beaming Cat looked, maybe it was because Will was too far away to reel me in—but something inside me snapped. All my mixed emotions were coming together like particles in an atom or exploding star, and were about to combust inside me. All the confrontations with Jason, all of his belittling of others, all of his schemes and sliminess, finally rose to the surface and boiled over. This straw broke the camel's back.

I decided today *would not be* the day the slimy Jason stole Cat's ideas while taking all the credit, not while she is busy spinning at a charity event she helped put together. Cat was thrilled all of her co-workers came out to support her, never expecting one of them to stab her in the back when she wasn't looking. *Not today, buddy, not on my watch.*

I could feel my mouth opening, the venomous words charging toward my teeth, scampering to get out. Every ounce of goodness inside me was saying, "I'm too nice, I don't want to rock the boat," but it was getting overrun by the rage of injustice. I said, perhaps even yelled, over the music to Phil, "You know, Phil, I want to make sure you're not misled. Obviously I didn't hear your conversation with Jason, but I know those ideas were actually Cat's. She has all the mock-ups and designs in her desk, which she can show you come Monday. I want to make sure she gets credit for her ideas, and I think she is a real talent. She mentioned it to all of us today, and Jason was there, and maybe he mentioned they were from her when he discussed the ideas with you, but in case he didn't, I know you like to be well informed Phil—and have all the facts."

I tried to sugarcoat it with a sweet-as-apple-pie smile, and a light touch on the arm. Sure, maybe I was taking advantage of the trust he had in me from winning the Milan PP account, but I firmly believe in using an edge when it is for a good cause.

Phil's look said it all: disbelief, anger, shock, bewilderment, unease, uncertainty, and disgust. A couple drinks sometimes can magnify the slightest emotion, and Phil was several drinks deep, probably adding to the severity in which he judged the situation. He also didn't want to be taken as a sucker, and as much as a good ol' boy he is, he also knew the value in finding intelligent, capable females who are bold enough to take on this dog-eat-dog man's world. Having a female lead on the account could be a leg up over the other competitors, especially if, like Cat, she was truly the person behind the brainpower and vision on an account.

"Well, thanks for letting me know, Liz, and you're absolutely right. I do like to be informed on all matters. Your candor is appreciated, and let your friend Cat know I want to see her first thing Monday morning to look over her folder. Enjoy the drinks, and tell Cat I think this is one heck of an event." He winked, handed us our drinks, and walked off to mingle. He was back to his suave unruffled self, and as a man who prides himself on always knowing what is going on in the office, he didn't stay too long talking about something he didn't know.

Yes, it was a risk being honest with him, and probably it would not have paid off if I hadn't won the Milan account. Thanks again to Will for choosing me, for I knew my words to Phil would hold their weight in gold. Now Phil headed back over towards Jason, the number of cocktails consumed must be fueling a confrontation. Dustin leaned in closer, "Do you think he is going to tell Jason directly what you said? If so, it is going to mean bad things for you, Liz." I swallowed hard, knowing Jason was a bit of a loose cannon, but what was the worst he could do? Watching them as I talked with Dustin, I saw Jason start to look agitated, and kept running his hand through his greasy hair as he used his other hand to gesture. He kept shrugging, and was looking a little green, and Phil walked away without his usual pat on the back. Jason, scanning the crowd, saw Dustin standing next to me, and made a beeline towards us.

"I think you're absolutely right, Dustin, unfortunately I think Phil told him everything because here he comes, and we are going to witness the wrath of Jason." I scanned the crowd looking for Will, but couldn't find him anywhere. My palms were getting sweaty as a feeling of unease came over me, as I wasn't exactly sure what to expect from this type of confrontation.

Jason approached us in a major huff. "Do you know what you just did, Liz? Do you? Phil is no longer considering me for my promotion because of *what you told him*." Jason was seething, his chest heaving with every breath, his eyes looking bloodshot and slightly crazed.

Breathing deeply, I said, "I don't know what you're talking about Jason. Phil simply started talking to us about Cat's ideas, and he somehow was under the mistaken impression they were your ideas. Now how do you think he got so confused?" I grinned very slightly, I knew it was wicked, but I couldn't help myself.

"Just you wait Liz, you're on my list." When he leaned forward toward my ear, I tried pulling back, but with the crowded bar I had nowhere to go. His breath was hot and tingly on my ear as he whispered, "You have made *a very big mistake*, and let me tell you Liz. I'm like a snake, and I will strike when you least expect it." He stormed off into the crowd. Dustin raised his eyebrows at me while I took another sip of my beer.

"What did he whisper to you? He did not look happy, Liz, the way he stormed out of here made him look more devilish than ever," Dustin said, as he watched Jason disappear into the crowd.

As I sipped my beer, I wondered if I had crossed an invisible line into full-out war with Jason. My face was starting to feel hot from the exchange, and my body was getting a strange tingly sensation. My gaze fell on my beer, where I saw something floating near the bottom. *What are those little blobs at the bottom of my beer? Yuk, super gross!* I was about to take my beer to the bartender to ask what extra item came along with my drink order, when the items at the bottom of my drink began to take shape, much to my horror.

I gasped, realizing there were small fragments of peanuts in my beer. Jason was munching on peanuts earlier. Did he know about my peanut allergy, and intentionally dropped a peanut in my drink as he leaned in tell me I was now on his list—and to watch out?

As I started to feel lightheaded, I looked up at Dustin. "Dustin, I'm not feeling so great." I mumbled as everything started to spin. I could feel my feet giving way beneath me as I felt myself fading. "Oh crap," I whispered, next thing I knew I felt someone grabbing me as I was falling. My eyes opened to see Will's strong arms, and a look of pure panic written all over his face.

"Lisette, are you okay?" I could hear him saying, but it sounded so far away.

"My beer," my voice echoed, sounding like it was coming from someone outside my body, and not me. My voice sounded foreign as I lay in Will's arms. Dustin was now holding my beer, which he must have been able to grab before I fell.

"Are those peanuts in her glass? Isn't she allergic?" I heard another voice say from the crowd before everything faded into blackness.

CHAPTER 19

Waking up, I was in the backseat with Will, and at first, I thought I was dreaming some sordid summer dream involving back-seats trysts and leather chairs, but his stone-like expression told me it was not the case. "How are you feeling, Liz?" Will asked roughly, his hand lightly touching my face as he peered into my eyes.

"What happened, Will?" I was still foggy and unsure of exactly why I was in a moving car, and why I was waking up. I noticed my leg was aching, and I wondered what I did to it.

"Someone dropped peanuts into your drink, and you had an allergic reaction. I used an EpiPen, so your leg might be sore for a while. We are on the way to the hospital right now, Doffing is driving us." With his words everything came flooding back. EpiPen? How did he have an EpiPen?

Seeing the cap from the EpiPen in the car's center console, I asked, "Will, not only did you manage to catch me from a nasty fall, but when last I looked, you were across the room. You completely saved me. You really are my hero. How exactly did you just happen to have an EpiPen?" I leaned my head against the cool leather seats, taking in his perfectly sculpted face and features. After my recent scare, it felt good to be with the living again, and to see him was comforting.

Will's hand went to the back of his head in a semi-stretch as he bashfully looked up at me. "I picked one up once I heard you had this allergy. Remember, I told you I wouldn't let anything happen to you on my watch. Call me extra cautious."

I could hardly be mad, or think it was a foolish precaution, because his foresight had saved me. I should really have one on me at all times, and as it turns out, I never know when someone will slip peanuts in my drink.

"Wow, I don't even know what to say." My head was still swimming, and I was starting to feel horribly embarrassed about fainting in front of all of my co-workers.

"You don't have to say anything, I'm so glad you're back. You really had me scared back there." He studied my face, as he placed a hand on the small of my back. With one quick movement he pulled me in close, arm over my shoulder as I rested my head on his shoulder. It was a comforting feeling being nestled so close to him. His body heat radiating through me, helping me feel more grounded after a trying last hour. I felt dwarfed surrounded by his strong arms and chest. I felt safe until I realized with a sinking feeling we were getting close to the hospital.

"I'm honestly fine now, thanks to you. We don't have to stop in the hospital," I mumbled against his chest. I was exhausted from the evening's turn of events, and right now, my body hated me.

"Not a chance, I want to make sure you're okay. Plus, we need to get another EpiPen, since the one I had has been used." His voice showed his concern, and I knew I wasn't going to get out of it.

"I must look like death warmed over," I murmured, feeling worse than I must look. "Naw, you look like a ray of sunshine. I was so relieved because you gave us quite the scare, Lisette." He cupped my face in his hands, and kissed me softly. I sighed, for being there with him made everything seem more bearable.

Luckily the doctor visit went by fairly quickly. Will spent a lot of the visit pacing outside my room on his phone.

He insisted we go back to his loft so I could rest up there. Exhausted, I played with my hospital wristband as Will paced in the room. It was time to come clean on everything that had gone on with Jason, and all the difficulties I had with him.

Will stood, he sat, he paced, he frowned—all while I told him about the run-in at the Falcon, our conversation with Phil, the time Jason came to my desk and told me he thought I was sleeping around to get to the top, the sleazy thing he pulled with the Judsons—and every other run-in. "Then tonight, Will, Jason's temper tantrum, and the fact I saw him eating a handful of peanuts before he walked up to me— all this led to the possible conclusion that Jason dropped peanuts into my drink intentionally, knowing full well about my allergy."

"So you really think Jason dropped those peanuts into your drink? Lisette, at the vineyard you promised to tell me if you had anything bothering you. How can I protect you like this, when you won't be honest with me?" His ocean-blue eyes, oh, I could hardly look at the pain and hurt behind them. I knew *I had screwed up*.

"I didn't want to worry you, and I didn't want to run to you with little insignificant things. I already knew I had an enemy, and I knew if I told you about him, you may insist on doing something about it to protect me, and I didn't want to make anything worse. Plus we were being so careful about making sure no one knows about us, I didn't want you to feel like you had to interfere. This situation between the two of us could come out, or make people suspicious. In hindsight, yes, maybe I should have said something, but I didn't realize he would *try to kill me*. What if he dropped it in my drink by mistake? Please tell me you understand, I can't have you mad at me on top of everything else," I pleaded, looking up at him.

"Of course, I'm not mad at you, Lisette, you almost died back at the bar. None of this is your fault, and I want to make sure you know it. Come here." I stood and gladly took one of his amazing bear hugs, feeling warm and safe within his embrace.

"Will, I just can't believe Jason is capable of trying to hurt me on purpose. Can you? I knew Jason was a jerk of varying degrees and proportions, but murder or intentional harm is a whole other level."

"Well, he knew his charade was up about the project,

pretending the work and idea were his when they really were not. He knew Phil would never look at him in the same light, but instead as a thief. Stealing intellectual property in this business, an idea or a pitch, is serious. Those ideas are what make careers. Phil had us all convinced to add him as an executive in the team, but it certainly won't happen now. We may not be able to prove he deliberately dropped the peanut in your drink, but we know he knew about the allergy, and we know he had motive to sabotage your career."

"Maybe we can prove it. I need a couple minutes to confront him face-to-face. I know what buttons to push, and I bet I can get him to admit to it. All of this speculation won't mean anything without proof, and I know I can get it." I peered up at Will—I was sick of this feeling of not being able to control anything that happened to me.

Will sat down next to me. "Liz, I understand your frustration and the desire to take back control, but I can't have you do that. Not only do I care too much about you to let you face this guy alone, but from an HR perspective, I can't agree to you approaching him if I believe there is a chance that he tried to kill you. You have more guts than anyone I know to even want to confront him after all of this, but I would knowingly be putting you in danger, and I can't do that. However, our hands are not entirely tied, and although we may not be able to prove intent, I am going to put him on probation because of everything you told me. He will have to take some unpaid time off, to get his head on straight, and explain himself. I don't want him anywhere near you after this. I will connect with HR first thing tomorrow morning to see if we can force him to pass a psych test in order to return to work. Let me worry about that; you should get some rest now."

Will kissed me lightly on the forehead, and when he pulled away, I grabbed the bottom of his soft shirt. "I don't know if I can fall asleep right now, with everything swimming around my head. Can you help me forget, to block it all away, for a little while?" He peered down at me intently as I gave him what I hoped was my seductive gaze.

"You want me to distract you from your thoughts, so you can finally sleep? Hmmm, I don't know Lisette. From the ordeal you have experienced, I don't know." He reached out and gently touched the side of my face, and leaned in for a soft, supple kiss. I pulled him in closer and breathlessly kissed back, passion erupting inside me.

"The way you handled everything today, and took care of me, I find it all so completely sexy, Will. And I can't get enough of you. Help me take my mind off everything. All I want to think about is you touching me, and your body against mine." Releasing my hair from its messy bun, I let it fall down my shoulder and back. His eyes looked dark with lust, I knew he wanted to take me here and now, but was debating if I was strong enough. In one swift motion he lifted me up in his arms and carried me to his bedroom, placing me softly on his dark silk sheets.

"We are going to do it my way, slow, so I make sure you're okay. I have the best thing to get your mind in the right place. Do you trust me?" he asked, offering a mischievous look.

"Yes, do with me what you will," I replied back playfully. He dimmed the lights in his room, and lit a couple candles giving the room a soft glow. I stripped to my tank top and boy shorts, and relaxed on the bed. Will took off his shirt, abs bulging as he sprawled out onto the bed next to me.

The candles were filling the room with an alluring scent. He leaned in close, saying, "I mentioned a little about delayed gratification before, I think tonight is the perfect night to play around with that to make sure you're up for all of this activity. Do you trust me enough to let me use your scarf to cover your eyes?" He was kissing my neck and nibbling my ear lobes, causing me to squirm on the smooth silk sheets. He pulled out the scarf I had tossed in my purse earlier, turned on soft classical music, and brought the scarf to the bed.

"Oh yes, I trust you." My voice deep and raspy, I was already starting to feel the familiar stirring of desire with him lying half naked beside me, lavishing me with soft kisses. He lightly put my scarf over my eyes, and moved my hands to hold the posts on his headboard.

"Stay right like that Lisette, and think *only of* the sensations." Soft classical music playing in the background added a sense of tranquility to the darkness around me.

He laid next to me, and I felt what only could be described as a feather or something soft and somewhat tickly, running slowly up and down my body. He covered my mouth with his as he ran his hand down between my legs, and applied delicious pressure and slow movement. He started kissing every square inch of my body, from my collarbone down to my stomach and hips, all the while slowly moving his hands and lightly caressing me with the feather, causing my body to move and react as I grasped the poles of his headboard and twisted with anticipation. I moved restlessly with the unyielding feeling of need, thirsting for him, with each touch leaving me wanting more. My breath was coming quicker as I writhed under his hard, taut body.

"Expect a new sensation in a moment, Lisette, breathe in and out, this one may surprise you a bit." I could tell he was smiling while he spoke. I gasped as I felt something shockingly cold and wet. He was slowly sliding ice from my lips, down my neck. It was sensual and erotic, and created a new, wondrous sensation. He was swirling the ice on my skin, and then masked the cold with the incredible warmth of his lips as he traced the ice path. Sucking and swirling his tongue, the stark contrast between the ice and the warmth of his mouth, was causing my whole body to react with the sensation of the changing temps. I was grasping the silk sheets, rolling the fabric into tight knots as he took me to the brink. I gasped, unable to take the sweet torture for much longer.

"Almost Lisette, almost, one more thing I want to try first. Remember, it is called delayed gratification for a reason." I could hear the grin in his voice as he moved on top of me. He spent time giving attention to every inch of my body as I lost myself in him, and each beautiful moment, as time slipped away. I lay gripping the bars of the headboard, the bittersweet pain of waiting to have him completely captivating my thoughts until I couldn't take it any longer. Groaning, I arched my back with pleasure as we made desperate and passionate love, finally collapsing into the sheets together. Removing my scarf, he tossed it on the floor as he laid next to me.

"Did I keep your mind off everything but the sensations, Lisette? Hope it wasn't too much for you." He had a lazy grin as he propped himself on his side to gaze down at me. I placed a hand on his chest, etching the lines of his protruding muscles with my fingers.

"Hmmm, yes. You did your job very well, Mr. Duke, and yes, my mind was absolutely focused on only you and the moment. Too much for me, no, I think it was absolutely the right amount. However, I am finally succumbing to pure exhaustion, and I think I could use some sleep." I stifled a big yawn as he nodded, and pulled me close to him.

"Just lean into me, doll, and you'll fall right asleep. I promise." He murmured, his voice also laden with exhaustion. I did what I was told, snuggled up to my man, with his arm around me. Those were the words I fell asleep to, and mercifully had a night of dreamless sleep.

CHAPTER 20

The doctor had cleared me to go back to work after some rest, so Will and I fell into a little routine in the mornings, first grabbing coffee, and then taking separate cars into work to avoid any suspicion. I had to admit I was enjoying the whole crashing at his place, maybe a little too much. And I wasn't relishing the thought of going back to my apartment any time soon. I thrust myself back into my work to keep my mind off things.

After grabbing a morning coffee with Cat and Dustin, and assuring them I was fine from the whole peanut situation, I was ready to get back to the routine. I didn't mention my thoughts that Jason was the one who dropped the peanuts in my drink, and when they started to ask about how the peanuts ended up in my drink, I excused myself to get ready for a meeting, and changed the topic. They seemed satisfied enough with my responses for the time being, but I knew eventually they would want to discuss it further.

While I was trying to get organized for the week, I eyed a non-descript padded envelope on my desk, dropped there with my other mail. It had no return address, and my name was in bold letters. My phone vibrated as I inspected the outside of the envelope.

A text read: *Welcome back to the office, lovely, swing by my office when you have a minute. I could use some sunshine. – Will*

What a charmer, and I smiled at his thoughtful note. I was excited to see him, even though we had left his place only hours ago. I could hardly get enough of him these days, and decided as soon as I got through my mail and some housekeeping cleanup with my emails, I would stop in—or sooner, depending on how long I could continue to focus, and make myself stay away.

Turning the envelope over in my hands, I became rather curious because I hadn't ordered anything to be sent directly to my office. As I slowly peeled it open, a letter and some large pictures popped out. I gasped when I caught sight of the contents. Inside were several candid blown-up photos of William Duke and Phil Burns, each with different women.

First I looked at all the Phil Burns photos, him with a hand on a model's butt, him hugging different gorgeous women, and overall schmoozing with a variety of gorgeous women. Then I started thumbing through the pictures of Will. In each shot he was adorned with gorgeous models draped over his shoulders and arms. One model in particular was a stunner, and I noticed in several candid shots with him she was wearing skimpy dresses and other glamorous model attire. Suddenly I recognized her face. It was the same model, the one in his office who I saw get a kiss and a hug from Will. There were somewhat compromising pictures of Will kissing her forehead and cheek. His arm was wrapped around her waist in a casual way, they were obviously very close and comfortable with each other in the photos, unaware someone nearby was taking snapshots of their activities. I tried to swallow the sick lump forming in the back of my throat. Was Will dating all of these women, and has he been dating them all this whole time?

Yikes, we never had the official "talk" about being exclusive, so maybe this was my fault to assume we were anything more than casual friends who hooked up. I mean, we didn't have rings on our fingers, right? I tried explaining it to myself, but it came back to one hard truth. I must view us as something different altogether than how he views us. How can you blame him? You could have me, or a gorgeous supermodel with zero percent body fat and flawless skin and hair. It doesn't take a rocket scientist. My thoughts started to spiral into more cynical streams. *What, so you thought you were special, Liz? You thought your Superman would really settle for you, when he can have someone like her? You never discussed it. He could be having sex with multiple other women, and you wouldn't know. You're a fool Liz, a fool for falling for someone like him. A playboy, a charmer, the Duke, honestly did you think this would end with the white picket fence?*

I squeezed my eyes shut, trying to concentrate on breathing to make sure I didn't pass out right in my office chair. Jealousy was swimming around my stomach. It was an avalanche of emotions all at once, I felt cheated, I felt betrayed, I felt angry, and I felt worthless. I suddenly started feeling very silly—maybe the magic between Will and me was something I had completely mustered up in my own imagination. Maybe I made something casual into something more serious in my mind. Yes, he has been there through some really tough times in my life, but maybe I mistook his compassion and his Good Samaritan attitude as something more—like an exclusive love, between two people. But obviously from looking at these photos, he had a connection with women up and down the business and model district. Maybe this should be his new slogan: Work with me and chances are I will sleep with you. *Wow, did I feel dumb.*

True, you shouldn't text when you're angry, but I couldn't stop myself. I decided I wouldn't have time to stop in and see Will today, and a text would be all he gets from me.

Will, I'm sure you're busy. You don't have to check up on me, I'm fine and I'm sure you have more pressing things to do, like proof some model shots, or schmooze more new business clients. Maybe we will run into each other later this week. – Liz

The moment I sent it, I felt like a bitch. I knew he would know immediately from my text something was wrong, but right then, I didn't care. So what if I found out he was going behind my back with a slew of other women, it was about time I knew. At this moment, my emotions were driving me, more so than logic.

I glanced up to make sure no one was looking my way, and I continued to look through the contents of the envelope that mysteriously showed up on my desk. More importantly, who sent these to me, and why?

Taking another look at the Phil Burns pictures, they featured him in a variety of scenarios with women. Behind the number of photos, was a folded letter. A sick feeling was developing in my stomach as I guessed what could be in the letter. In generic computer print it read:

You slut, see what your two admirers really think of you. Did you know about their other ladies? Maybe you're not as special as you think you are, LIZ, they are just using you. You think they would care if something happened to you? Think again.

Maybe you should find another job, or another place to live. Your roommate seems to think she should stay at your current place, so maybe you should change her mind before something bad happens.

If you're thinking of ignoring this letter, contemplate this. Will you be able to live with yourself knowing you could have saved her? Time is ticking, Liz, and don't dream of telling your "boyfriends." Go to your place now, go alone, don't tell a soul, or "say goodbye to your roomie forever".

My eyes burned and tears flowed as I read the letter again, my hands trembling. The person who broke into my house must have grabbed the two notes from Phil and Will, and from those notes, assumed I was somehow involved with both men, and sent me photos showing them with other women.

Why, and for what purpose? To raise doubts in my mind, to get me scared enough and angry enough to go to my place alone to make sure my roommate was okay? They had succeeded, I was absolutely shaken and feeling deflated. My relationship with Will was not what I thought, and now my roommate might be in trouble because of me.

When I tried calling Jodi, it went right to her voicemail, so I left a shaky message asking her to give me a call back as soon as she was able, saying it was urgent. My mind raced, considering my few options. The person who was targeting me paid special attention to the people I knew, running this type of surveillance on Will and Phil, this took time on their part, and it made the whole letter that much more intimidating to realize this also required some patience. Whoever was behind this was obviously calculating, and he made it clear I couldn't go to anyone for help. Nor could I run to Will in this case, being he was a focal point of the photos. Now I realized I couldn't rely on him like I thought I could before. I didn't want to be the obnoxious girl who kept asking the guy she was seeing to do things a boyfriend should do, because obviously he didn't see me that way. I couldn't help but wonder if I was girl number one, or three, or five on his list? How did I measure up with the line of beauties he had on his arm?

Then the realization hit me, I had no other choice but to head to my old place to see if Jodi was there, and to warn her, knowing full well this could be a trap. The letter had worked, and I couldn't dare to risk telling anyone for fear of Jodi's safety. I couldn't tell Will because the photos of him and the other women were burning in my mind. I didn't have the luxury to dwell on my own personal wreckage. I had to go by myself, and I had to go now. I reached down into my bottom drawer and took out a can of mace Will had suggested I buy after the first break-in, and put it in my purse. I shuffled all the photos and letter quickly back into the manila envelope, and shoved it down to the bottom of my purse. I felt like a lamb heading to slaughter, but I took a deep breath and started toward my car.

CHAPTER 21

When I pulled into the driveway of my place, and glanced at the windows, it looked dark and uninhabited. I grabbed the mace from my purse, and tentatively approached the front door. Opening it slowly, I noticed the lights were off, and no one seemed to be home. *Oh my, was Jodi trapped somewhere, or had someone already got in, and tied her up?* I started calling her name as I walked through the rooms. Satisfied she wasn't hidden away, I started to leave, the mace grasped tightly in my hand. As I was walking towards the front door, I heard tires screeching down the block. Quickly I raced to the bathroom in the back where I'd have a better view of the street. I watched a large red truck speeding down the street—with something long and black sticking out of the back window.

Explosions like firecrackers erupted all around me. I dropped to the bathroom floor, glad to be towards the back of the house. I could hear metal clanging on the tile floors of the kitchen, and peering through the open bathroom door, I could see tuffs of cotton stuffing from cushions and pillows peppering the air as bullets whizzed through my living room. Terror seized me as I realized I was getting shot at, and someone was driving by, shooting real bullets through my doors and windows. Frozen on the floor, I listened as the tires peeled away. Once again silence surrounded me.

My phone was vibrating in my pocket, and I quietly pulled it out. *Could this be the same person who sent me the letter, now calling me to see if I was still alive?* I knew I had to get out of the house in case they came back. It took every ounce of personal resolve to get my brain to react. *Move Liz, get out of the house, they could come back to finish the job. Get your legs to move Liz, move NOW!*

I shot up from the floor, and bolted towards the back door, my phone in my hand. I didn't know exactly where to go, but I knew I had to run somewhere. There was a pile of trees sort of blocking the path leading into a woodsy walking path. If nothing else, the shooter or shooters couldn't drive a large red truck through the blocked path, and at least I would see their truck coming. I made a mad dash towards the trees, hoping I didn't run into anyone trying to kill me on the way.

CHAPTER 22

I felt like I was in high school again, running through neighbor's backyards, and around fences, not daring to go on the main streets for fear of getting caught. Time seemed to be passing in slow motion. With all of the running, my breath was coming out hard and fast, chest aching because my lungs were not used to sprints, and I looked over my shoulder every few minutes. My heart was slamming in my chest, and throbbing in my ears.

When I was satisfied I was safely hidden from view from the main road, I collapsed on the ground behind several rows of trees. Checking my phone, I saw the missed call was from Will. I pushed the button to call him back, and he answered.

"Liz, where are you? Max told me you dashed out of the office suddenly, and your text didn't seem like you, is everything okay?" My eyes were pinched shut, I was trying to catch my breath, and he could undoubtedly hear my panting.

"It...is... a... long story," I gasped, "I went back to my place... I went there to find Jodi... they shot up my place, Will!" Deafening silence filled the other end of the phone. Would Will berate me about the foolishness of going back to my place by myself?

"Stay put, I'm coming to get you," Will said in a steady, determined voice.

"Okay, let me try to explain where I am." I could feel tears starting to gather around the corner of my eyes. *Keep it together Liz, don't crumble now, you're not safe yet.*

"I know where you are, I took a chance and checked the app that Max installed on your phone to locate it in an instance where it is lost or stolen. You didn't change your password yet, so I lucked out. I was able to get in and track your cell's location," his steely voice came back, and I could hear murmurs sounding like Max in the background.

"You did? Wow, good thinking. Glad I didn't get around to changing those passwords." I exhaled with relief, and glad Max put that application on my phone.

"Yes, you can thank Max and me later," he replied, his voice sounding rough now. It was a pompous response, typical of my hero knowing what I needed before I needed it. Was it his paranoia, or did he see the whole situation escalating before I did? I couldn't help but feel relieved. He quickly told me to try to hide myself, and said it would be better if I wasn't talking on the phone but was hiding in silence in case anyone was still looking for me. Begrudgingly I hung up the phone, I knew he was right, but my hands were trembling as I cut off my lifeline, and retreated farther back from the road, into the coverage of the forested area.

When Will pulled up on the side of the road and led me safely to the car, I could finally breathe again. He explained they were able to contact Jodi, and she would have police protection until they figured out who was threatening us. Relieved, I sunk into the soft leather chair, and I wanted to talk to Jodi to simply hear her voice, but since the police were busy questioning her, and looking for clues as to who was behind this madness, I would have to wait.

Driving to the lakefront property in Winnetka didn't take as long as I expected. I was still on an adrenaline high, and could hardly sit still in my seat as Will drove. He kept glancing over at me, probably to make sure I was not going to scream my head off in some sort of delayed response to the shock of the shooting. The mix of jitters and a haze of disbelief kept me silent as we drove.

"We will be there soon, you will be safe there, Lisette. I promise," Will said, and he gently took my hand and kissed it as he kept an eye on the road. I kept blurting out different suggestions for things I could do to help find this psycho who was chasing me. I hated this feeling of helplessness, and I wasn't used to people doing things for me—anyway, not before Will.

"I know you want to do everything you can to find this person, Lisette, but right now the best way you can help is to let me in. I can keep you safe, and I have people who can help the police do the legwork we need while keeping you out of harm's way. No one is viewing you as helpless. You were lucky today, if you were standing in the living room or anywhere else, a bullet could have easily found you. I don't want to risk giving them another shot at you. Let me help." He looked over as he squeezed my hand, and I nodded with a hard swallow.

He filled me in on the fact that he had pulled together his driver, Doffing, and Max to work with the police, and to figure out who could be causing all of this mayhem. Finally I came clean with him on the red truck I saw when I went to visit Jodi, and the red truck she thought she saw driving by our place shortly after the whole Ben situation. I described Ben's skull tattoo on the back of his neck, but it didn't add up as to why someone who had a brief, yet humiliating interaction with us would become so fixated.

I had expected Will might chastise me for not telling him all of the details earlier, but to my surprise he didn't say a word. It made me feel a little better to be able to contribute something that could help in the investigation. Afterwards, he made a lot of calls to Max and Doffing, requesting them to do some digging. He especially wanted Doffing to look into who had originally invited Ben to the event at the bar during our company outing where Jodi met him. Did he live in the neighborhood, or was close by, or did he have another connection somehow.

As we sped towards his lake house, a place I had only heard of in passing, I tried to concentrate on my breathing. I looked over at Will, steely-faced and determined, white knuckling the steering wheel as he took occasional calls from his staff—and I was in awe of my real-life Superman, in the flesh, and I drank in the moment.

It was the only moment all day when I felt my heartbeat finally slow down a little from its previous feverish pace.

I had to keep sneaking glances at Will to remind myself I wasn't dreaming, I had successfully escaped from whoever was trying to kill me, and for the time being I was safe.

My mouth dropped as we drove into the curved, gated driveway of his lake house, which looked more like a mansion than an actual lake house. After pulling into the four-car garage, we took a quick tour of the grounds. There was an expansive in-ground pool in the back, with a view of the lake down below that you could easily access via the stone walkway. The inside of the home was breathtaking, warmer and more casual than his loft at the heart of the city, but equally as painstakingly decorated. The cathedral ceilings let in a lot of beautiful light, and windows looked over a gorgeous deck out back. The place was massive, and the tour of each room left me feeling like I could absolutely get lost in a place like this. The grounds led to a couple other buildings out back, and occasionally I would see a groundskeeper or someone who was part of the family staff walking around, tidying up, but it didn't seem like any of his family was there. He explained part of the house was for private use, so we wouldn't have to worry about anyone intruding on us where we were staying. I was amazed—what wealth it must require to own a place like this. I would have asked a lot more questions, but my mind was still on the bizarre twist of events from which I just escaped, with the help of my own lovely Superman.

Once we got settled at his lake house, Will called the police to let them know where I was, and explained why we left the city. When Will explained the situation, and the fact that someone was obviously trying to kill me, they advised us to stay at Will's lake home until they could send someone out to meet with us. They also were sending a uniformed police officer to check out the damage at my place due to the drive-by shooting, and to investigate further.

After the call with the police, I dug the manila envelope containing the photos and letter out of my bag to show Will as a way of explaining the whole situation, and why I ended up back at my old place without letting him know. My hands were shaking slightly as I filled him in on all the details. I also told him about seeing him with the model in his office, and then receiving those pictures verifying what I thought.

"Jeez, Lisette, why didn't you tell me?" His expression was pained, holding the pictures in one hand, the note in the other.

"Is this why you left the office without telling me about this whole thing, and why you sent me that text? You saw these photos, and assumed I have been seeing multiple women at the same time I've been with you?" Agitated, he paced the room while looking at the incriminating photos strewn about the table.

"I…I could hardly think. Obviously the person who broke into my place took both the notes from you and Phil I had sitting on my desk, and thought I was involved with both of you, or wasn't sure which one, so included both to hedge their bets. I know the pictures were supposed to make me question whatever relationships I might have, and it did. To be fair, we have not talked about being exclusive or anything else, but yes, I have to admit I was jealous. My mind was racing from the note and the photos, leaving me angry and confused. Will, you don't have to explain those photos. We are not exclusive, and are having fun, so honestly, you don't have to go into it."

Will came over to me, gently lifted his face to mine, and delicately kissed my lips.

"Liz, you should have told me. I'm surprised you don't know by now the *only* one I want is you. I can explain each of the photos; some of these are candid pictures from the advertising photo shoot in Florida. This means the person who sent you these photos either knows someone, or works within our own company." He was holding my hands steady as he spoke, and I couldn't stop them from still trembling under his warm hold.

"The girl you see in the majority of the pictures, the one who came to my office you saw me hug, the same girl I am kissing on the cheek with my hand around her waist, is my half-sister. No direct relation to me except my father was briefly married to her mother. I try to get her modeling jobs with the company whenever I can, but don't like to broadcast the family connection. We are close, but I view her as a sister, and she views me as a brother. We have that type of love for each other, which is why you saw me kissing her on the cheek and hugging her, and why you see me with her in the majority of these photos. No one knows about the family connection other than Max, Doffing, my house staff, and now you." He was pacing around the room, as if he was debating telling me something more.

"Half-sister, your father was married to her mother for a period of time. Wow." I was relieved, and yet stunned by the news. While trying to control my breathing, I felt like I was constantly spinning with him—and was somewhat saddened by how little I knew about his family and prior circumstances. I decided to be daring, and ask what I really wanted to know.

"Is your father Mr. Bradley, as in the Mr. Bradley of Burke and Bradley?" Startled, Will turned towards me. "Please don't say anything to him, but Doffing mentioned something about working with your dad previously when we were at the vineyard when he was about to drive us home," I said tentatively, and watched Will's jaw clench.

"Doffing should know better than to let something like that slip." He was about to pull out his cellphone to make a call, undoubtedly to make sure such a slip never happens again.

"Will, stop! I asked him some questions; it was not his fault. You were about to tell me yourself anyway, so please don't bring it up to him. Yes, I have known about Mr. Bradley since the vineyard, but I didn't say anything. Yes, I maybe should have told you about the letter and pictures, and the reason I freaked a little from seeing you with your half-sister in your office, but I didn't want to seem foolish and petty. Then when I received the photos in the mail, I hate to admit it, but it raised reasonable doubts in my mind. I wondered why you would want me when you can have any one of those beautiful women.

"However, I take full responsibility for rushing out of the office to tackle this myself when I obviously couldn't handle it, but Will, you didn't even tell me your dad's name is on our agency, and he *owns* the company. I don't know anything about you personally, and you're surprised I don't believe I'm the only girl in your life. I feel like you don't trust me enough to show me who you really are, so how am I supposed to trust you? Then I received those photos, plus I thought my roommate was in danger. The time and effort someone spent to get those photos is a another disconcerting piece, these people are somehow internally connected, and out to get me. Why is this happening to me, I don't get it!" Tears started to well up in my eyes.

"Hey, hey it's okay," he said gently. "You're here with me now, and you're safe. I'm not going to let anything happen to you, okay? I promise. Do you believe me?" He said the last piece with a little smile as he kissed my cheeks. I nodded. "You also believe me when I say I don't want any of the girls in those photos. You don't realize how incredible and sexy you are, Lisette. I'm frustrated you don't see how special and desirable you are, but I will make it my mission to convince you."

"You're *also right*, Liz," he said roughly, "I should have been honest with you about my father. I have worked so hard to separate myself from him so people don't think I got where I am today simply by trailing on my father's coattails. Changing my last name to my mother's maiden name, Duke, I built up a reputation and career on the assumed name. I didn't want anyone to know, because I want people to respect me for me and my accomplishments, not for my father. It's more of a pride issue, than trust, I have been living behind the image I built for myself for so long I'm not used to letting people in." He peered at me to gauge my reaction, and continued, "I also don't date. I'm a confirmed bachelor, and I never date a girl seriously enough to bring her in to my family or friends, or share my background. Until now that is, with you. It is not a trust issue, with you I'm in uncharted territory, Lisette. I can tell you one thing though." He crouched before me, and his strong hands took mine as he looked me in the eye.

"I have never experienced the panic and the pain I did when you left the office, and I had no idea where you went, only to find you were shot at, and your life put in danger. The feelings I have for you, Lisette, are getting stronger every day, and I want to let you in. I need to let you in, because it would kill me to think you don't trust me. I can't explain this feeling I have towards you, I need to protect you, and it tears me up inside to know someone is after you, but I promise you I will work harder at letting you in, and bringing you into my world. I already brought you into my home, so this is a first small step." He gave me his full Duke smile, and then I was putty in his hands again.

Oh, so that is why when I Googled him nothing appeared before his tenure at Burke and Bradley. It was because he took on a different name, and so of course nothing exists online before that change.

"My dear Lisette, come here." The intensity in his gaze sent shivers up my spine—it was lustful and primal. I took it all in, his familiar striking features, and knowing eyes looking down at me. I tried to capture the moment forever as a memory I didn't want to forget. He seemed larger than life in the darkness of the room, silhouetted with the glimpse of the pool lights seeping in through the white curtains. I felt a swirl of warmth in the pit of my stomach for I had never wanted him so much. I rushed up to him, enfolded in his embrace as our momentum pushed us against the wall. His hand pulled my leg up by his waist, our bodies flush with one another. I needed him, needed to devour him, and forget everything else.

Will pulled back to look at my face, to check my expression to make sure I was mentally okay to be intimate with him, but right then, he was my cure—my distraction, my safe harbor, my rock, my Superman—my hero. I craved his lips, sucking them gently as my hands searched his hard chest muscles and shoulders. I felt him lift me, my legs wrapped around his waist as I kissed his neck and face. My breath coming quicker now, he lifted me and placed me gently on his satin sheets, while I was desperately pulling at his clothes. Right now, I needed him to shut out my other thoughts.

"We can slow down, Lisette," he murmured as I masterfully undid his belt, and yanked it out, throwing it and his shirt to the floor by his pants. I stood up from the bed so I could be face to face with him

"No, William, I can't slow down. Lately I feel like my life has been anything but normal, and I want some normalcy. I want to be able to love, and not have to worry about getting shot at, or poisoned, or fed misinformation. I want to feel like a normal woman, and *you make me feel better than normal.* You make me feel extraordinary, which is what I need right now. I need the good things in my life to overshadow the bad I have experienced lately. Everything about you is good, and we can go fast or we can go slow, but I need to be with you right now. You remind me I'm still here, still alive, and finally safe." Gazing into his concerned eyes, I could see he was deep in his thoughts, and deep in the momentum of all the recent chaos, but I wanted to pull him out of that so he could be present with me, here and now. I stood from the bed so I could be closer to him as he considered my words.

"Just be with me," I whispered, as I nibbled his ear, and kissed him deeply.

His hot breath grazed my neck, and turned to light kisses on my tightly closed eyes. Withering under his touch, I was becoming impatient. My lips fervently asked for more as we pushed up against the wall. I didn't want to wait to get back to the satin sheets; I wanted him now. I guided him inside me, as we braced ourselves against the wall, straddling him as he lifted me, pushing my back against the hard surface, my legs wrapped around his waist. My hands clutched and clawed at his back with each thrust, head thrown back in ecstasy as he easily held my weight against the wall.

My thoughts focused only on the fire between us, and the swell of pleasure he created whenever he touched me. It was a fiery moment of passion, each of us desperately needing the other, to remind ourselves we made it through this together, depending on each other, and dissolving into one another as if nothing else existed outside of this bond.

"I want you, Will." So close to the point of exhilaration, I was begging him to continue, but then he would stop and pepper me with kisses. His hot breath on my skin, mixed with his eager movements, was a heady mix of sensations as we continued discovering each other. I gripped his strong back as my breath came quicker.

"Open your eyes Lisette, look at me." My eyes snapped open on command, his eyes darkened with lust. I ran my hands through his hair, biting my lip as I struggled to keep his gaze, and we continued moving together in sync. We were reaching a feverish pitch, and together found the indescribable swelling of bliss, satisfying the hungry itch to have him completely.

I collapsed into him, his strong arms wrapping around me as he carried me over to a large comfy sofa. He sat beside me, and I snuggled into the wonderful spot at the base of his neck and shoulder where my head fit perfectly, draping my legs over his. I was still shaking slightly from the whole ordeal of the day, but hearing his heartbeat was helping to calm my nerves. He pulled me in close, and absentmindedly ran his fingers through my hair.

He must have been reading my mind, because every once in a while he would say, "You okay? I would never let anything happen to you ever. I love you, Lisette." My breath caught. I pulled back and looked at him, at those piercing blue eyes ripe with emotion. I smiled, beaming at him, the happiest I felt in a long time. "I love you, too." I replied, and snuggled back up to him."

The next couple days at the lake house went by in a whirl. Doffing, members of the police department, Max, and others were constantly coming in and out of the house. I tried to keep myself busy, but felt a little useless as everyone else worked to put the pieces together for me. Finally, the news broke.

Doffing and Max arrived at the lake house to bring us up to date, having already filled in the police on what they found. They located Ben and his red truck, they identified him by using the security cameras in the ramp across the street from Jodi's store, and using security footage from the store he walked into that day. They confirmed Ben was the guy who drove past our apartment the day Jodi thought she saw a red truck, and the same guy who followed me to Jodi's store in the parking ramp. They identified the bullets at my place as matching with the type of gun he owned, and found the notes from Phil and Will at his place. The real surprise was his connection to Burke and Bradley.

"I started digging into how he met you and Jodi at the company event at the bar the night Will had to kick Ben out of your place," Max said, his sleeves rolled up, pacing as he talked around the room. I went back to the bar, and knowing the manager gave me an opportunity to use a favor to dig into some of their credit card receipts to get his last name. There had to be connection to someone at the company, since he had those candid photos of William and Phil. This is where Doffing came in. We worked together to uncover the connection."

Doffing was sitting on the arm of the large sofa, arms folded. He cleared his throat to begin, "I started to dig into known associates, where he hangs out, his circle of friends, and networks on social and business networking sites. It turns out he had a lot of the same connections as one of your very own at Burke and Bradley. They were smart enough to not be directly connected, but we were able to figure it out with some crafty work from Max." Doffing paused for effect as we all waited. I was sitting on the edge of the chair about to explode from nerves.

"Your buddy, Ben, is the second cousin to Jason Dean from Burke and Bradley. Jason is the one who invited Ben as his guest to the bar the night of the work event, the one where you invited Jodi as your guest, and she ended up meeting Ben. Ben was there as Jason's guest. Once Jason learned of the connection Ben made with Jodi, he decided to pay Ben for his services to keep an eye on you. Ben has a prior record of vandalism, breaking and entering, and a ton of petty-theft charges. Jason paid Ben to stake out your place, and brought him in on his whole scheme.

"Jason became dangerously fixated with getting an

executive spot at the company, but Liz and Cat stood in the way. Once you won the competition at work, Liz, you made his list. He thought scaring you with Ben breaking into your place, and writing the ominous note stating he is watching you, would be enough to put you off your A-game, and he could horn in on the action and get a promotion. He thought he could weasel into a top spot, but when you got the nod anyway and good things kept happening to you, he realized he had to take it further.

"When you effectively stopped him from stealing Cat's ideas, he had to take you out of the picture before you did more damage. He *was* the one who dropped the peanuts in your drink. Knowing you were the only person who could effectively piece together the fact he was the one with opportunity to drop peanuts in your drink, and could accuse him of it afterwards, he had to make sure you could never rat him out. He thought the severity of your allergy would be enough to land you six feet under. Luckily, William had an EpiPen on hand, and could quickly administer it, which allowed you to survive the whole ordeal. Of course, this meant you were still alive and able to further ruin his reputation with Phil. Once you conveyed your thoughts to William about Jason poisoning you, and William ordered the psych test, Jason snapped. He ordered Ben to shoot up your place, hoping to hit more than cushions.

"The police put a rush on the psych test results William had ordered, and it turns out Jason is a certified sociopath bent on criminal behavior to get what he wants. He is singing like a bird now, trying to put all the blame on Ben. They will both be locked away for a long time, so don't you worry. Knowing this ties up all the loose ends regarding who targeted you and why. With everything we uncovered, this should be an open-and-shut case, which means both of the bad guys will get their due." Doffing smiled, and Max nodded.

Pleased with their combined efforts and outcome, Will shook both their hands. "Great job guys, thanks for all your hard work and effort on this." I hugged them both and extended my heartfelt thanks. I told them I'd forever be indebted to them for putting away two dangerous men who could have ruined my life.

"Are you kidding? We are happy to help William with whatever he needs, but this stuff sure gets the blood pumping. We are so glad you're safe, and we could help in a meaningful way. We are going to run over to the police station to give our statements, and let you two get some rest," Doffing said, as Will walked them to the door.

Slumping back in my chair, I was exhausted and overwhelmed by all the crazy news. Will came back in the room, smiling, his deep voice cutting through the fog of my thoughts. "You look like you could use a joke right about now."

I rubbed my hands over my eyes. "Yes, I think I could right now."

"They opened a new restaurant down the road called Karma, but they don't have a menu, you simply get what you deserve." He chuckled softly as he fell back onto the sofa next to me.

"Haha, how fitting," I mused. "Well, I guess this all means I can move back into my old place now," I said, putting my hair up in a high ponytail.

"Lisette, there is no rush. Plus, I don't know if I like the idea of Jason knowing where you live, whether he is behind bars or not. Why don't you stay with me for a while? It has worked out great so far?"

Sitting up on the sofa, giving him a bewildered look, I asked, "Are you serious? You mean like move in with you? Will, I don't know." I twirled my thumb ring anxiously.

"Yeah, I mean there is no rush to find another place. You could move in with me while you look, and if you find something, great, but if you don't, you can just stay. I love you Lisette, and I want us to be together. This way each day I come home I'll know you're safe, which is a comforting thought after this whole ordeal.

"One good thing came out of fear of losing you is that I can no longer deny how much this shook me at my core. My feelings for you are too great. I want us to be exclusive, and I want to start introducing you to my family and friends. You were right, I was too closed off from all of those years of experience, but I don't want it to be like that anymore, not with you. You don't have to worry, I don't mean to overwhelm you with everything all at once, but we can figure it out. We can take things slowly, but I want you to be my girlfriend, if you're willing." His chest rose as he took a big breath to wait for my response.

"Oh my gosh, Will, I don't know what to say," I stammered, wondering if I was dreaming, or still in shock from the whole Jason scare. *Did I hear him correctly? Officially be his girlfriend, live with him until I found another place, if I found another place, and meet his family and friends? Like a normal relationship, with Superman?*

"Lisette, please say yes, and we can figure it out together." His eyes were pleading with me, and he pulled me in close as he waited for my reaction.

"Will, what about Burke and Bradley, wouldn't everyone find out?" I asked, thinking about the disapproving stares.

"Well, I have thought about that long and hard. I guess now is as good of a time as any to bring it up. I was going to talk to you about an opportunity I think you might enjoy. I was talking with my father, and he is looking to open an office location in Milan to have a central location in the European market, which would also be a great central spot for the Prescott Pine account. He would like me to help occasionally with the project, and I could use a consultant to help with the opening of new business branch.

"How would you like to be the outside consultant, Lisette? This would remove any direct HR opposition to us dating, and we could still reveal our relationship to HR. It is a great resume builder, and it would allow you to travel with me on new business initiatives. You wouldn't have to worry about giving up copy writing, as there will be plenty of work to be done at the new office. I was thinking of giving Cat the executive spot Jason coveted, and you would be able to consult with her on anything she needs. What do you think?" Will anxiously read my face. Shocked, but delighted, I couldn't speak, but lunged at him for one of his famous big bear hugs.

"Will, yes, yes and, yes. Pinch me, I must be dreaming. This sounds amazing. I don't know what else to say, I'm stunned, but incredibly excited. I mean, would your dad want to hire me in that capacity though?" I could hardly breathe because my heart was beating so fast, and I thought I might never stop smiling.

"You will have plenty of time to meet him, but I already told him about you, and he thinks it is a great idea."

"Wow, I don't know what to do next, I feel so incredibly lucky. Not only am I relieved and grateful to be alive, but also lucky that all of these twists and turns have led me to you. I feel like I'm about to jump out of my skin. What do we need to do now?"

"Eventually, we will want to grab any your stuff from your old place, and bring it to my loft in the city. Since the police are still sifting through everything, we have some time. For right now, we can relax, take some breaths, and enjoy the moment. We have all the time in the world to figure it out, doll, no need to hurry."

As he gave me one of his heart melting smiles, I leaned over to give him a long, deep, smoldering kiss. I curled up next to my Superman, and smiled because for the first time in a long time, it felt like everything was going to turn out okay—no, better than okay.

THE END

ACKNOWLEDGMENTS

First, to the authors who impacted me throughout my life, your work has touched the lives of many, and brings such joy to book lovers everywhere.

To my wonderful and talented beta readers and extra editing eyes, you women are fantastic, and I can't thank you enough for your time and guidance. Thanks Susan, Ann, Jenna, Michelle, and Sherri—your insight and suggestions helped me make this the best version possible. Ann, all of your printing services and support are phenomenal. Susan, a special thanks to you for fielding all the extra calls/texts/emails along this journey, you have helped me so much, and wrote a beautiful endorsement for the book—I am eternally grateful.

Huge thanks go to Connie Anderson, my editor extraordinaire, whose endless humor, wisdom, and editing magic helped me turn this book into something special.

I would like to thank Alan Pranke for his beautiful cover, and for the way he crafted the design for the interior of the book. You surpassed my expectations, and I am so pleased I had a chance to work with you.

Kassy, thank you for your photography genius, what you are able to capture through the lens is tremendous. Also special thanks to Michael, for opening my eyes to that which I could not see.

A special thanks to Erik for taking the time to share your experiences, the path to publishing, and for introducing me to the resources I needed to complete this project.

To the amazing and empowering Women of Words (WOW) group, thank you for bringing me into the family. I am continually inspired by this amazing group. I always look forward to our time together.

I want to thank my family who raised me to chase each and every seemingly impossible dream. To my parents, whose loving support encouraged my sister and me to create stories, songs, and plays, which is part of how I caught the writing bug.

A big thanks to my husband for giving me the freedom to pursue my passions, for your amazing chef skills on the days I was attached to my computer writing, and for your sense of humor as we take this journey together.

I also have to mention all of the talented and hilarious friends and family who always encourage me to be myself, and to pursue my dreams. Please know your unwavering faith in me was fuel to the creative fire.

I owe everything to my faith which has brought me to where I am today, and I am grateful for each moment. I feel truly blessed.

ABOUT THE AUTHOR

C.E. Sawyer is a longtime fan of the romance genre, and finally discovered how much fun it can be to write her own. Writing is more than a passion for the author—it is a true addiction. As a lover of books, and an avid reader, she graciously thanks all the authors who have inspired her throughout the years, and hopes her work will give that same joy to her readers and fans.

C.E. Sawyer lives in the Upper Midwest with her husband and puppy. Her favorite thing to do during the long winters is to grab a cup of strong, steaming coffee, and work on her latest writing project. She is on a mission to create her own library of works, and is currently working on her next novel.